Rudra Veena

An Ancient String Musical Instrument

By
Pandit Hindraj Divekar
"B. Com, Surmani, Sangeet Vadan Kala visharad, Pandit, Sangeet Shree, Hind gandharva Shree, Been Bhaskar, Dhrupad Shree and Pune Gaurav"
Dr. Robin D. Tribhuwan
M.A, MSc, Ph.D, Post Doctoral Fellow

2001
DISCOVERY PUBLISHING HOUSE, NEW DELHI - 110002
(INDIA)

First Published-2001

ISBN 81-7141-581-4

Published by
DISCOVERY PUBLISHING HOUSE
4831/24, Ansari Road, Prahlad Street,
Darya Ganj, New Delhi-110002 (India)
Phone: 3279245 • Fax: 91-11-3253475
E-mail:dph @ indiatimes.com

Printed at: Tarun Offset Printers

This Book is dedicated
To
Late Hindgandharva, Pandit
Shivram buva Divekar

Noted Rudra Veena Player,
an actor and a vocalist
Birth - 1 - 4 - 1912
Death - 26 - 7 - 1988

Preface

India is an Anthropological laboratory, with its religious, linguistic, regional, cultural & ethnic diversities. Its musical tradition is no exception to the rule. In India one finds a variety of musical instruments and traditions. Many of these instruments are not known to people. Most of the musical instrument & traditions have died a natural death in the due course of time, while some of them have become rare.

These rare musical instruments and traditions need to be made known to people, hence their documentation is essential. In this book an attempt has been made to bring into light one such ancient stringed musical. instrument, the Rudra Veena. We have done justice to the book by touching essential aspects of this little known musical instrument, and its styles.

We feel that, this work will certainly evoke interest in many researchers and musicologists, to take up studies on little known and unknown musical instruments & traditions of India. The methodology evolved by us will certainly contribute in understanding other rare musical instruments & traditions. Its time for the researchers to dive in to the glorious parts of Indian musical traditions and bring out the valuable fragments to be made known to the present generation.

Pt. Hindraj Divekar

Dr. Robin. D. Tribhuwan

Contents

1

An Overview of Music and Musical traditions in India

(1.1) Concepts and Definitions of music :

Music is a basic social and cultural activity of man kind. It has probably existed in some form, from the earliest days of man. Man was born with a great musical instrument, his voice. He undoubtedly used his voice to express himself through music, long before he thought of making music with instruments. For thousands of years in man's early history, music existed only in simple and natural sounds. Music developed as time passed by. Today, composers write their music down using symbols, and performers can record their music on records or tapes.

Definitions of Music :

The oxford dictionary refers the term music, to an art of combining vocal and, or instrumental sounds in harmony and expressive ways.

Yet another definition states that, music as an expression of various moods, seasons and emotions, deeply apealing to the senses, music transports one from the mundane to the transcendental world.

According to Engel (1968 :564). "Music is an expression of inner life, an expression of feeling through the technique of compositon, according to the rules of a certain musical style. As expression, music affects the listener as well as the player. It liberates feelings, but it also demands, on the part of a listener, receptiveness and an acquaintance with the style in question".

(1.2) Salient Features of Music :

In his article captioned, Music, Robert C. Marsh (1981 : 785- 802) has classified certain characteristics of music. These are as follows :

(i) Music Produces Sound :

Sound in music usually has a definite pitch, that we describe as high or low. A musical sound called tone, is produced when something causes a series of vibrations that recur, a certain number of times each second.

(ii) Music Produces melody :

Melody is a succession of musical tones - in its simplest form, a tune.

(iii) Music calls for harmony :

The tones heard with a tone strengthens it and often helps set its mood. Composers harmonize music in chords, which are groups of three or more related tones sounded at the same time, there by creating a musical harmony.

(iv) Music has Rhythm :

Rhythm may be considered as everything that has to do with the duration of the musical sounds. Accent is an important factor in musical rhythm.

(v) Music has Tempo :

Tempo is the rate of speed at which music is played. It is related to, but not part of, rhythm. A change in tempo can often change the meaning of music.

(vi) Music & tone colour :

Tone colour is one of the most elusive qualities in music. Human voices may sing the same range of notes, yet produce widely different sounds. Different choice chords give varying colours.

(vii) Music has verbal or written language. Various instruments affect the tone colour of the music they play.

Every known society in the world has produced various styles of music and musical instruments. Let us now briefly look into the classification of musical instruments.

(1.3) Classification of Musical Instruments :

Almost all the musical instruments that can produce music can be grouped into three major classes : stringed, wind and percussion. They make sounds in three different ways. Vibrating strings produce the musical tones in the first group. Wind blown into or though a tube produces the tones in the second group. Something struck produces sounds in the third group. But because of the way most musical instruments are made, most experts divide them into six major groups. These are as follows :

(1)   Stringed Instruments :
Stringed instruments are of four basic types :

(a) Bowed Stringed Instruments : These types of instruments are bowed (rubbed with a bow) to produce sounds. Examples of these instruments are in violin family.

(b) Plucked Stringed Instruments : In the second type of stringed instruments, the players pluck strings to produce tones. They may use their finger as in playing a harp or they may use plecktrum, a small piece of ivory, wood, plastic or metal. Examples of plucked stringed instruments are Banjo. Guitar, sitar, Rudraveena, Lute, Lyre, Mandoline, Ukulle, Zither etc.

(c) Hammered Stringed Instruments : Here the string is hammered by the musician to produce a tone. Examples of these instruments are piano. Clavichord, Dulcimer and the Santoor - an Indian classical instrument.

(d) Wind Stringed Instruments : In the fourth type of stringed instrument, the strings vibrate in the wind. The only instrument of this type is the harp. It is never used in orchestral music.

(2) Wood-Wind Instruments :

These instruments are grouped together because at one time they were all made of wood. Today they may be made up of metal or plastic. Wood winds instruments produce tones, when the musician blows air into or through a tube, either directly or part a vibrating reed. Some examples of these are flutes, wooden clarinets etc.

(3) Brass Instruments :

All brass instruments have rather long bores (tubes) with mouth pieces at one end and flaring bells (openings) at the other end. Many brass instruments have values that serve to lengthen or shorten the tube, lowering or raising the pitch.

For instance, the horn family has a narrow, conical bore, with a funnel-shaped mouth piece and a large bell. The trumpet family has a narrow, cylinderical bore, a cup shaped mouth piece and moderate size bell.

(4) Percussion Instruments :

These include all instruments that have key boards connected with a mechanism for producing tones. Instruments like organ, cynthesizer etc. may be categorized in the category.

(5) Key Board Instruments:

These include all instruments that have key boards connected with a mechanism for producing tones. Instruments like organ, cynthesizer etc. may be grouped in the category.

(6) Other Instruments :

Some reed instruments have free reeds that vibrate back and forth in a slot. They include the accordian, concertina, harmonica, and harmonium.

(1.4) Concept of Ethnomusicology :

The decipline of Ethnomusicology provides detailed studies of the construction and tunning of instruments, as well as a precise classificaiton of instruments according to the mechanism of sound production (aerophones, chorodophones, idiophones and membranophones).

Human societies world over have developed ways and means to compose a musical style, thereby giving rise to little and great musical traditions. By little traditions we mean primitive or tribal musical traditions, while great traditions are those which have been recognized as formal traditions and are in textual form. The tribal music in India, for that matter may be categorized into little musical tradition category, while the Hindustani and Karnatak musical traditions befall in the later.

Musical sound does not and cannot constitute a system that operates outside the control of human beings. It is thus a product of human behaviour, includes a wide variety of phenomena, but within the rubric of four particularly important facts can be seggregated. They are :

(i)   The physical behaviour of the musician and his audience.

(ii) Social behaviour that accompanies music.

(iii) Music needs training.

(iv) Verbal behaviour involved in music.

In other words, before music behaviour can be acted out, there must be underlying concepts in terms of which the behaviour is shaped.

Every musical instrument and or tradition has cultural rules, styles. Behavioural musical tradition of "Rudra Veena" of the Hindustani classical Indian music is no exception to the rule. This book tries to unravel the history status, change and continuity of the musical tradition of Rudraveena, keeping in view the following aims.

(1.5) Aims of the Book

(1)   To highlight the concepts and definitions of the terms music and ethnomusicology.

(2)   To present a brief history of Indian classical music.

(3)   To bring into light the historical, socio-cultural, theatrical and musical status of "Rudra Veena - An Ancient String instrument".

(4)   To highlight the efforts of those unknown and little known players of Rudra Veena, also known as the masters of sound and silence, to preserve and popularize this vanishing musical instrument and its style.

(5)   To unravel the role of Rudra-Veena makers & well wishers to preserve, promote & propagate, this vanishing instrument.

(6)   To suggest a plan to policy makers, administrators and music institutions to preserve and popularize this instrument.

Before getting into understanding the historical, sociocultural and musical aspects associate with Rudra Veena. It is necessary for our readers to understand a brief history of musical traditions of India.

(1.6) Status of Indian Music from Pre-vedic Period to Modern Era :

(A) Pre-vedic period :

The origin of music in India is attributed to Gods and Goddesses and to mythological figures like Gandharvas and Kinnaras, who figure stories and legends connected with the science and practice of music.

According to Joshi G. N. (1977 : 6) one legend states, that lord Brahma the creator, taught classical music to Lord Shiva, who gave it to Saraswati, the Goddess of learning. Hence, Saraswati is described in ancient texts as "Veena Pustaka Dharini" (one who has the musical instrument veena and a book in her hands). From then on, music came to be handed down, in succession, to the Sage Narada, the celestial Gandharvas and the Kinnaras, Bharata and Hanuman, who came to earth to propagate it among people.

According to another legend. Lord shiva made a gift of music to Narada a reward for his penance (tapasya). Once when Lord shiva saw his spouse Parvati in a reposeful pose, he was inspired to create the Rudra Veena (a specialised stringed instrument of the Veena type) and from out of his five mouths in five directions emanated the five ragas : "Bhairav" from the East, "Hindol" from the West, "Megh" from the South, "Deepak" from the North and "Shri" from the sky above. To this list the one added by Parvati was known as "Kaushik".

Yet another legend quoted by Joshi G. N. (1977 : 6) says that Lord Shiva was so enamoured of Parvati that he made her sit on a throne and expressed a desire to dance before her. All Gods also joined him. Saraswati played on the Veena, Indra wielded the flute. Brahma played the Kartaal, and Lakshmi stated singing to the accompaniment of the Mridang played by Lord Vishnu. According to yet another legend, Lord Shiva gave music to bharata. Thus, the diverse legends have one thing on common, namely, that the art of music had divine origin.

References of musical instruments excavated from Mohanjodaro and Harappa sites, cave paintings and sculptures found in Ajantaha, Ellora caves, the Konark temple (sun temple) of Bhubaneshwar, the Khajuraho temple, the Huddukka sculptures etc., reveal the tradition of Indian Classical Music is very old. Even traditional ancient scriptures namely Samaveda and later on the epis of Ramayana and Mahabharata have references of musical instruments and traditions.

(B) Vedic Period :

The vedic period of Indian history is usually attributed to the entry of Aryans in India, some where around 2000 B. C. Some sociologists believe that caste system in India, was given birth to by the Aryans. To maintain their superiority over the Dravidians, Aryans promoted caste system in India.

With the introduction of caste system occupational and social responsibilities were bestowed on communities and concerned individuals. This perhaps paved a way for certain caste groups only, to take up learning the art of music, dance and performing sacred rituals etc.

The art of music was passed on from one generation to another in certain families, popularly known as Gharanas, today. This is how the art of music was preserved right from the vedic period right up to present times.

It is written that the early form of vocal music was known as "Samagan", which is derived from the term "Sama" - meaning melody. Initially there were only three types of notes namely Udatta, Anudatta and Swarita, out of which developed the other four, thus completing the octave, in Rigveda, for example one finds mention of the Veena, the Vanshi (flute) and the Damaru (small drum). The technical classification of Udatta, Anudatta and Swarita in Samaveda is given as below :

Udatta		Anudatta		Swarita		
Ni	Ga	Re	Dha	Sa	Ma	pa
7	3	2	6	1	4	5

The Buddhist and Jain scriptures also contain reference to jati music, also some crude sketches of Veena. Around 400 A. D. The great poet. Kalidasa wrote his Abhijana Shakuntalam. Which clearly shows an attempt at blending poetry with classical music.

The epics, Ramayana and Mahabharata, were written during 500 B. C. To A. D. 200. In Mahabharata there are reference of the seven notes

Sa	Re	Ga	Ma	Pa	Dha	Ni
1	2	3	4	5	6	7

While the Ramayana tells us about Ravana, the demon king of Lanka, was a great musician and that when Lakshmana, Rama's brother entered the inner chamber of Sugriva, the monkey king, he was enchanted by sweet music of the Veena. Also in the battle scenes of both the epis, the names of various Indian classical musical instruments, such as the bheri, the dundubhi, the mridang, the ghat, the dum-dum, the mudraka, the veena etc. are found.

The Natya shastra, witten by Bharata, during A. D. 400 to 500, is the first and most dependable evidence to be found regarding the basis of Indian classical music. It was Bharata who first gave the names to seven notes of the octave. According to Hindu philosophy the Natya Shastra is regarded as the most authentic book of drama and classical music.

According to Bharata Muni, a musician is responsible for evoking a particular emotion or mood which he called "rasa". He enumerated eight such emotional states and gave to each a presiding deity and a colour equivalent. These Nava-rasas, nine basic emotions, are fundamental to Indian aesthetics. They are as follows.

Sr. No.	Name of Rasa	Nearest Equivalent	Deity Associated	Colour Associated
01.	Shringar	Love	Vishnu	Light Green
02.	Hasya	Humour	Pramatha	White
03.	Karuna	Pathos	Yama	Ash/Grey
04.	Rudra	Anger	Rudra	Red
05.	Vir	heroism	Indra	Light Orange
06.	Bhayanak	Terror	Kali	Black
07	Bibhatsa	Disgust	Shiva Mahakali	Blue
08.	Adbhuta	Wonder	Brahma	Yellow
09.	Shanta	Serenity	Narayana	White

During the time of Bharata hermit the seven notes (saptak) were classified as Shadja, Rishaba, Gandharva, Madhyama, Panchama, Dhaivata and Nishada. They were known by initial notes known as Sa, Re, Ga, Ma, pa, Dha, Ni. These Indian notes correspond to the Western scales C, D, E, F, G, A and B. The seven notes or swaras were associated with sounds of birds and animals. They are as

Sr. No.	Note	Bird/Animal	Pitch
01.	SA	Peacock's Cry	Sa to Sa
02.	RE	The cow calling her calf	Sa to Re
03.	GA	The goat's bleat	Sa to Ga
04.	MA	Singing of birds or cry of the deer	Sa to Ma
05.	PA	The song of the Kokila	Sa to pa
06.	DHA	The Horse's niegh	Sa to Dha
07.	NI	Trumpeting of an Elephant	Sa to Ni

Bharata's son Dattila is also credited with one book captioned "Dattilam". Another writer Matanga, wrote a treatise Known as the "Brihadeshi", around 8th century in which we find, distinct mention of the term raga. Reference is also made to the seven grama-jat is which were then in vogue and in which there was one known as Vatta-raga-jat. About the same time or may be little earlier, another Narada wrote the "Naradiya Shiksha", which gives a description of seven grama-ragas.

Thus according to Joshi G. N. (19 : 7), the period from A. D. 400 to 1100 shows that music made considerable progress. It appears that the Jatis were subsequently consolidated into six principles basic melodies and soon afterwards, two branches of classical music were ushered into existence : the Northern or Hindustani school and the southern or karnatak school.

(C)   Indian Music During Moghul Period (About 1100 A. D.) :

Books on Indian classical music were written in Sanskrit language, it was hard for them to understand the same. They gradually developed great aptitude and interest in indegenous music. Their interest in evinced by the fact that Muslim musicians introduced new musical instruments and evolved quite a few new molodies. About this time (A. D. 1210 to 1247) "Shrarangadeva" - a great musicologist at the court of Yadav kings of Devgiri, wrote his celebrated treatise "Sangita-Ratnakara" which gave a sound and scientific basis to music. The author has also attempted to develop theoritical insights into both Hindustani and Karnatak musical traditions. This book is the first publication to discuss the Ragas in detail and developed its list up to 264 ragas. This book also presents the concept of time and appropriate raga to be sung or played during a particular time.

A system of notation has also been outlined in "Sangita-Ratnakara", known as Srutis. Their names are as follows :

(1)   Tiwara, Kumadvarti, corresponds the note Sa

(2)   Dayavati, Ranjini, Rattika for the note Re

(3)   Rudri and Krodhi for the note Ga

(4)   Vajrika, prasarini, preeti and marjani, for the note Ma

(5)   Kshiti, Rakta, Sandipini, Alapini for the note Pa

(6)   Madanti, Rohini, Ramya for the note Dha

(7)   Ugra and Kshobini for the note Ni

From the classification given above, it is evident that the parent scales Shadja-Gramma had gained ground by this time. A slight set back to the Hindustani music in North India is evident in the first half of the century because of constant military encounters between the ruling Hindu princes and the invading Muslim forces.

In the latter half of the century, the famous poet musicologist, Jayadeva's book written in Sanskrit, namely "Gita Govinda" made its appearance. The songs in this book were mostly descriptive of the loves of the cowherd God lord Krishna for Radha and the milk maids.

After the Muslims settled down they turned their attention to Indian art and culture. However, it was during the reign of Allauddin Khilji (A. D. 1296 - 1316) that music received a great fillip. At his court there was a Minister by the name Hazrat Amir Khusro. Hazrat Khusro's greatest contribution to the field of music is the invention of the most popular stringed instrument, the 'Sitar' and the pair of drums known as Tabla.

Yet another musician by the name Nayak Gopal is also a legendary figure in the history of Indian music. He was attached to the court of Allaudin Khilji.

Towards the 15th century another writer by the name, Lochana wrote a book called the "Raga Tarangini". During the later half of the century Sultan Hussain Sharqi (A. D. 1458-88) patronised the Khayal style of singing and also evolved several new ragas, such as Jaunpuri - Todi, Sindhu - Bhairavi, Rasili - Todi, Sindhura and like.

The credit for introducing the dhrupad style of music goes to none other but, Raja Mansingh of Gwalior. The famous dhrupad exponent Nayak Baksu was attached to his court. During this time the bhakti (devotion) movement became famous in North India.

In the 16th century, during the reign of Emperor Akbar (A. D. 1556-1605) music in India may be said to have truly reached its zenith. Akbar was a great connoisseur of art and culture, particularly classical music. Although Akbar's reign is considered to be very glorious for Indian music, that of his Jahangir (A. D. 1605 - 1627) was no less eventful.

Notable musicians like Tansen, Baiju Bawra, Ramdas and several others were in the court of Akbar. In fact Akbar had as many as thrity six experts in the field of art and music employed in his court. Contrary to the encouragement given to musicians by Akbar and his son Jahangir, Emperor Aurangazeb (A. D. 1658 - 1701) as an enemy of classical music. Thus, while the Muslim rule was responsible for the flourishing growth of art and music, the seeds of its decay were also sown during the same period.

(D) Indian Classical Music During The British Rule :

After the Muslim rule, the Britishers came to India in the garb of traders and liasoned relationships with rulers of native states of India. They gradually and eventually succeeded in wresting power from the native princess.

The period following the subjugation of India by the British, presents an entirely different picture. It marked a gradual elimination of the old and cultured mobility. In the changed conditions, ruling princess became very indifferent to art and artists, except in few cases, where some did appoint state musicains. The rising middle class was too observed with its problem of livelihood.

They had therefore no other means to do anything for the promotion of art. To the poorer and profane masses, traditional music had long, remained a sealed work. The history of the first three decades of 20th century, therefore saw a complete route of the art and artists from the social stage of the nation.

It was at this critical juncture that two illustrious persons, endowed with remarkable vision and ability, appeared on the scene. These two were Pandit Vishnu Narayan Bhatkhande and Pandit Vishnu Digambar Paluskar.

Pandit Bhatkhande was a great scholar. His monumental work of compilation of thousand of musical compositions from all over the country and the printing of these, with notations brought an immense treasure knowledge within the easy ready of music lovers.

Where as Pandit V. D. Paluskar was a great performing artist. He toured the length and breadth of the sub-continent, popagating the art and expounding its greatness. With the zeal of a missionary, he converted millions of apprenticeears into good listeners of music. He created galaxy of artists, and established music schools in major cities.

The work of both pandits during the British reign, deserves praise, because it represents the first successful attempt at the revival of ancient music. Music to both was a gospel of God and they preached it to people. Their names will certainly go down to the annals of music in India.

(E) Indian Classical Music After Independence :

On 15th of August, 1947, the British rule over India, came to an end. For the first time in several centuries, Indians became free to shape their destiny in a democratic set-up. With the formation of the Central and State Governments, a number of schemes were taken up to safe guard the interests of Indians. Promotion and preservation of traditional calssical music was no exception to the rule.

Institutions like the Sangeet Natak Academy, established at the centre, with its branches all over the country. Many Colleges and Universities introduced classical music and other traditional art forms in their syllabus.

Scholarships were offered to students having outstanding talent. Cultural delegations which included musicians as well, were sent abroad, to propagate Indian classical music and other art forms. Titles and awards were conferred on artists of disinction and merit. Both State and Central Governments set up Ministries for cultural affairs and annual festivals in music, dance and drama to promote the interests of masses in arts.

Late Pandit Jawaharlal Nehru, the first Prime Minister of India, took a lot of interest in preserving and promoting Indian classical music and other art forms as well. He honoured general stalwarts in music and other fields. This was certainly an inspiration and encouragement to the artists.

(F) Status of Classical Music in The Modern Era :

With the spectacular advance made in the fields of scientific research and invention, it has brought phenomenal changes in the habits musicians and players as well. Television, tape recorders, radios and other communicational devices have given a new dimension to the enjoyment of music. Listeners can hear as well as see the musician playing.

The establishment of music companies have given rise to mass production of audio and video tapes and CD's. All most all great musicians of India, have recorded their audio and video tapes and CD's. A person who cannot attend or cannot afford to attend a live concert can consol himself by hearing or seeing the artist play on tape or V. C. R.

Yet another, interesting change that has taken place these days, that is most great musicians have registered music academies, to train the interested students, both in India and abroad. This has, certainly contributed in preserving and promoting Indian classical music both in India and abroad.

It has been observed that Westerners are getting attracted to Indian music. This has paved a way for some musicians and other artists to perform live concerts and conduct workshops in the West.

To conclude a note on the status of Indian classical music, there are two school of thought, as regards preservation and promotion of the same is concerned. These are :

(1) The first school of thought advocates preservation, promotion and propagation of classical music in its traditional and original form. That is without giving any room for syncritization.

(2) Where as the second school of thought advocates promotion and propagation of Indian classical music with syncritization. For example, combination performance of table with Western drums. Live performance of Sitar with Clarenet and so on.

In the process of change over several decades, some musical instruments and the concerned musicians were hidden or forgotten. Rudra Veena, is one such instrument which lost its glorious past, as time passed by. This research therefore, is turning point in the history of Indian musical research and aims at motivating research scholars and musicians to dive into the past and search the unknown and little known musical instruments, musicians and musical traditions of India.

(1.7) Significance of the Study :

As mentioned earlier this research aims to first of all motivate more and more musicians and research scholars to dig into the glorious past of Indian musical history so as to putforth the little known and unknown musical instruments, musicians and traditions, which remained in the dark. The study has certainly done justice to "Rudra Veena" - an ancient musical instrument, which was in the dark, has been brought into light in texual form. At the theoretical level, this study will provide new dimensions and insights to musicians an researchers to conduct more research on other aspects of Rudra Veena. For example, the Ethnobotanists can discover the process of growth of the gourds (species) and also the process of making the same. They can also figure out why and how the production of these gourds became extinct.

At the more practical level, this study aims to impress upon the policy makers and administrators associated with cultural ministries to draft out strategies to revitalize, the glorious past of Rudra Veena, by encouraging schools, colleges and universities and music academies to take up preservation, promotion and propagation of the great ancient musical instrument.

The book will certainly attract the attention of musicians, vocalists, researchers and students of Music, Fine art, Anthropology, Sociology, Ethnobotany, History and so on. It can be used as a base to conduct research on other little known and unknown musical traditions, of India.

2

Research Methodology

(2.1) Setting of the Study :

The present research work was carried out in India, as the origin and continuity of Rudra Veena - the ancient musical instrument is associated with the musical history of this country. Cities and towns which have nurtured the great musical heritage of Rudra Veena in India were visited so as to gather relevant data.

Thus. Pune, Miraj, Kolhapur, Ichalkaranji, Ahemednagar and Satara in Maharashtra ; Indore, Bharanpur, Gwalior, Bhopal, Mandav, Devas and the then province of Malva from Madhya Pradesh ; Jaipur in Rajasthan; Dharwad, Bangalore & Mysore in Karnataka; Lucknow and Agra in Uttar Pradesh; Delhi, Calcutta and other important places were visited by the authors, to interview musicians, makers of Rudra Veena, Drama Company owners and relatives of late Rudra Veena players.

(2.2) Target Population :

In order to gather scientific facts about "Rudra Veena" and its musical tradition in India, it was imperative to interview the living players of Rudra Veena. Besides, this, relatives of late Rudra Veena players were interviewed too. To understand the status, change and continuity of "Rudra Veena" production, its makers were interviewed. In fact there is a separate chapter on "Makers and Well Wishers of Rudra Veena", in this book. Yet another category of respondents were owners of Drama Companies and well wishers of Rudra Veena. By interviewing the above mentioned categories of respondents, it was possible to present a holistic view of Rudra Veena.

(2.3) Method of Data Collection :

Since the book aimed at unravelling both historical and current status of Rudra Veena, it was necessary to bank on both primary and secondary data. Thus, as mentioned earlier, primary data were gathered from present players of Rudra Veena and relatives of past Rudra Veena players, owners of drama companies makers and sellers of Rudra Veena and finally well wishers of the instrument were interviewed using interview scheules (see Appendix).

Secondly, data was collected from books, journals, magazines and other relevant published sources. Besides this nearly 39 diaries of late Shri Nata Srestha Chintoba Divekar, singer and eminent theatre actor-during the period (1886) to (1956) were referred and analyzed. This helped us in assessing the status of Rudra Veena, for over 100 years. Nata Srestha Chintoba Divekar Gurav passed on these valuable diaries to his son Late Hind gandharva Shivrambuva Divekar, who passed it on to his grand son Pandit Hindraj Divekar. These valuable diaries and the information in them was of immense help.

(2.4) Pandit Hindraj's personal Experience as Rudra Veena Player :

Pandit Hindraj Divekar, one of the Authors of the book and an eminent Rudra Veena player, who spend 35 years of his life learning an mastering the art of Rudra Veena, under the guidance of his father, late Pt. Hind gandharva Shivrambuva Divekar and his grandfather late Nata Srestha Chintoba Divekar, has contributed in presenting the technical and theoretical insights associated with the instrument. His experience of playing almost 260 Raghas on the Rudra Veena paved a way to develop the greatness of this classical Indian instrument.

Since he has been interacting with musicians of Rudra Veena, owners of drama companies, makers and sellers of Rudra Veena, his rapport helped the authors to gather relevant information about the instrument.

(2.5) Time Frame for Documentation :

It took fifteen years (1984 to 1999) for the authors to document detailed information on Rudra Veena. Pandit Hindraj Divekar dealt with the technical and musical aspects of Rudra Veena, while Dr. Robin D. Tribhuwan assessed its significance from Sociological, Anthropological and historical perspective.

The book is thus, a combination of musical as well as social Science efforts, making it an inter-disciplinary study. Considering the quality and kind of information in the book, it would be appropriate to state that this book will be of immense help, to not only musicians, but also researchers and students of Anthropology, Sociology, History, Ethnobotany, Ethnomusicology, Art and Cultural studies etc.

(2.6) Analysis :

The data gathered through primary and secondary sources was analyzed manually, as it was qualitative in nature.

(2.7) Chapter scheme :

This book in Presented in seven chapters. The first chapter Captioned, "An overview of music and musical Traditions In India," highlights concepts and definition of music, classification of musical instruments, brief history of Indian classical music, aims and significance of the book. The second chapter, Provides the research methodology used by the authors to gather, analyze & present the data Scientifically.

Third chapter namely, Types of Indian Classical musical Instruments, provides a brief account of some of the major string, rhythm, wind and side rhythm instruments of Indian classical music. The fourth chapter as the name suggests the Place of Rudra Veena in Indian classical music, focusses on the history of Rudra Veena, the masters who played Rudra veena, current status of Rudra veena, the way to play it, some lessons of Rudra veena & the styles of playing this ancient Instrument.

Just as the players of Rudra Veena who are becoming less & less day by day, so are the makers. Chapter five Provides a case study of the Rudra-Veena makers & its well wishers. The sixth chapter presents the efforts made by various people to presence, promote & propagate Rudra Veena. Finally the last chapter unveils conclusions from the data analyzed. It also throws light on certain policy decisions & actions to be taken to revitalize Rudra-Veena.

❏ ❏ ❏

3

Types of Indian Classical Musical Instruments

3.1 A Word About Indian Musical Instruments :

Sanskrit treatises on music and leterature containing references to musical instruments, begin from about the 3rd Century B. C. in Barhut, Sachi, Bhaja etc. The artists of ancient India have sculputured various types of musical instruments, in scenes depicting the life of Buddha. Varieties of Veenas, Flutes, Drums, pipes, Conches, Bells and Gongs are represented in the ancient sculptures (Krishna Swami, 1965 : 17),

Further, down the Indian history the muscial instruments mentioned in the literature during the Gupta period are the Vipanchi, the Parivadini (a seven stringed instrument) the Muraja (a type of drum), the Vasa (flute) and the Kwansya tala (stringed instrument). Kalidasa refers to Turya Vadya (wind instrument), Vallaki and Atodya and the Jalaja was a Conch sounded in war and peace and the Ghanta was a bell.

The period beginning from the 12th Century appears to have been a turning point for music and musical instruments in India. The Muslim rulers were great patrons of music. Some famous musicians were Amir Khusro a great poet and musician at the court of Sultan Allauddin Khilji. He did much popularize music in India. Khusro invented, evovled and introduced new styles of singing, new instruments, new talas and ragas. The invention of Tabla and Sitar, the qawwali form of singing and numerous ragas and compositions are attributed to him.

In North, Indian music reached the peak of its splendour during the reign of Akbar (1542-1605) who was a great patron of art. The musical instruments used at his court were been (Veena), the swarmandal, the Nai (Flute), the Karna (Trumpet), the Ghichak (a kind of Persian lute), the Tambora, the Surnai (Shahnai) and the Quanum (a kind of a swarmandal). Thus, the Muslims too were responsible for creating a number of musical instruments. It can be therefore concluded that it was the musical instruments which created styles.

3.2 Classification of Indian Classical Instruments :

Musicologists classify Indian Musical Instruments into four categories namely :

(1) Tata or String Instruments

(2) Vitata or Rhythm Instruments

(3) Ghana or Side Rhythm Instruments

    (4)   Sushir or Wind Instruments

Lets take a quick look at what kind of instruments fall in every category mentioned above. Secondly, for the sake of those readers who are strangers to concept of Indian classical music, we have provided brief description of some of the major musical instruments.

3.3 Tata or Stringed Instruments :

Some of the major stringed or tata musical instruments are :

    (a)   Been or Rudra Veena

    (b)   Veena

    (c)   Tanpura or Tambora

    (d)   Sitar

    (e)   Sur bahar

    (f)   Surshringar

    (g)   Sarod

    (h)   Vichitra Veena

    (i)   Rabab

    (j)   Gottuvadyam

    (k)   Sarangi

    (l)   Dilruba

    (m)   Mandar Bahar

    (n)   Esraj

    (o)   Santur

    (p)   Swarmandal

    (q)   Ektara

Table 3.1

Brief Description of Stringed Musical Instruments

S. No.	Instrument	Brief Description
(a)	**Been or Rudra Veena**	Been or Rudra Veena is the mother of all stringed instruments. It is considered to be the instrument of Shiva. Been consists of a bamboo fret board about 26 inches long and two and a half inches wide upon which are fixed on 24 metalic frets one for each of four octaves. The frets are fixed on the stem by a resinous wax like substance. This fret is mounted on two large gourds, each about 54 inches in diameter.

Rudra Veena has four main strings for playing, it also has three side strings. Of these two are on the left side, while one is on the right. Been is held in a slanting position on the left shoulder, the upper gourd resting upon the shoulder and the lower gourd on theright hand, the left hand passing round the stem and stopping the strings over the frets.

(b)   Veena

The Southern Veena consists of a large body hollowed out of a block of wood, generally jackwood. The stem of the instrument is made of the same kind of wood & the bridge is placed on the flat top of the body. The neck is attached to the stem and is usually cared into some weired figure like the head of a dragon. Another gourd smaller in size than the rounded part of the body is fixed underneath the neck and forms a kind of rest support to the instrument.

The Veena has seven strings in all. These strings rest on twenty four metalic frets, one for cad semitone of two octaves, are fixed on the stem by means of a resinous substance. The frests are arcs made of bell or of steel.

In order to play the Veena, the musician has to sit crossed-legged upon the floor and hold the Veena in front. The small gourd on the left touches the left thigh, the left arm passing round the stem so that the fingers rest easily upon the frets. The main body of the instrument is placed on the ground partially supported by the right thigh.

(c)   Tanpura

'Tanpura' also called "tambora," is one of the classical instruments and is usually a large one, ranging from ten inches, to one and half feet wide. The over all length of the instrument varies from 3 1/2 to 5 feet. The belly is usually slightly convex. The bridge placed on the bowl in the centre, is made up of wood or ivory.

There are four metal strings, three made of steel and the fourth and lowest one of brass.

The strings pass through holes in an edge near the peg. The tuning of pegs of the first and the second strings are fixed at the side of the neck ; those of the third & fourth are at right angles to the head. The strings are attached directly to the narrow edge fixed to the body.

There are beads threaded upon the strings, between the bridge and the attachment to which they are secured. These beads, pushed down in the direction of the attachment act like wedge between the belly and the strings, by thus streching the strings, they serve to alter the required pitches. This contrivance renders accurate tuning easier.

A tanpura player always holds the instrument upright with the body resting upon the ground in front of the performer. Sometimes the bowl is placed on the right thigh.

The player then, plucks the strings gently one after the other, in the same order. The finest tamboras are made in Miraj, Lucknow and Rampur in North. In the South Tanjavoor, Trivendrum, Vizianagram and Mysore are famous centres of manufacture.

(d)   Sitar

One of the most popular & commonest stringed instrument in India is the Sitar. Its body is made up of a gourd, cut in half near the core. Originally the gourd was almost flat, like the back of a tortoise and therefore such a Sitar was called "Kachchawa".

The finger board of the Sitar is about 3 feet long and 3 inches wide, hallow and deeply concave, covered with a thin piece of wood. There are sixteen to twenty two slightly curved frets of brass or silver. These are secured to the finger board by pieces of gut which pass underneath. This arrangement makes possible for the frets to move so that intervals of any scale can be produced.

Sitar has eleven or twelve sympathetic strings, which run almost parallel to the main strings under the frets. These are secured to small pegs fixed at the side of the finger board. The sympathetic strings are tuned to produce the scale of the melody which is being played.

A sitarist uses a wire plectrum (mizrab) worn on the fore finger of the right hand. The thumb is pressed firmly upon the edge of the gourd, so that the position of the right hand should change as little as possible. All the styles namely alap, jod, Jhala, meend etc. can be played on this instrument.

The invention of Sitar is commonly credited to Amir khusro, the great musician and statesman at the court of Khilji and Tughlak Sultans of Delhi, in the 13th Century. The name of Sitar is derived from the persian expression seh-tar meaning "three strings", Which is the number of strings the instrument had originally.

(e)   Surbhar

The Surbhar is actually a large sized Sitar. Its body is made up of wood with flat back. Its strings are thicker than those of the Sitar and the instrument is therefore tuned to a much lower pitch. The tuning and playing technique of Surbahar is just like the Sitar. The Surbahar is one of the fascinating instruments of North India.

Its invention is credited to the famous beenkar Omrao Khan, who later taught his son Sajjad Hussain There are very few players of Surbahar.

(f)   Surshringar

The Surshringar is the combination of three stringed instruments, namely the Mahati Veena, the Rabab and the Kachapi Veena. The small gourd and the neck to which the strings are attached are features of Mahati Veena, the finger board with a metal plate is very much like the type of rabab which Tansen played and the main body is similar to that of the Kachchapi Veena, popularly called Kachchapi Sitar, with its flat gourd resembl ing the back of a tortoise.

Sur shringar has six strings which are placed on a flat bridge. There are two aditional strings for the drone and the rhythmic accompany. To play it, the instrument is placed in front of the performer and held in a slanting position so that the upper portion rests on the left shoulder. The strings are plucked with a wire plectrums worn on the fingers of the right hand and the notes are with the fingers of left hand.

(g)   Sarod

Reference of Sarod is made with the famous musician of Akbar is court Tansen, who seems to have played the instrument then. Though built on the principle of rabab, the Sarod has few structural modification which make it suitable for the purpose of render ing all subtle graces of Indian music.

Its size Varies from 3 to 3 1/2 feet long. It is made up of wood. One end of the body is rounded nearly a foot in diameter and covered with partchment. The round part gradually joins the neck. There are six main strings including the chikari for the drone and rhythmic accompanyment. All the strings are metalic.

These strings are fastened to pegs at the neck end of the instrument. Some varieties have a small gourd attached to the neck end. The finger board is covered with polished metal plate to facillitate the sliding of the fingers while playing. The Sarod has 11 or 12 sympathetic strings which help to improve the resonance.

Sarod is played with a plectrum held in the right hand, while the fingers of the left hand are used for stopping the strings and playing notes. All characteric styles of instrumental music namely alap jod, jhala an meend can be rendered perfectly on this instrument. It is mainly a Solo instrument.

(h)   Vichitra Veena

The Vichitra Veena in general appearance & structure is very similar to the Northern Been or Veena. This instrument is not a fretted one. It has much broader and stronger wooden stem.

This hallow stem is about 3 feet long and about six inches wide, with a flat top and rounded bottom is placed on two large gourds about a foot and a half in diameter. An Ivory bridge covering the entire width of the stem is placed at one end. Six main strings of brass & steel run the whole length of the stem and one fastened to wooden pegs fixed to the other end.

The instrument has 12 sympathetic strings of varying lengths, which run parallel to and under the main strings. They are usually tuned to reproduce the scale of the raga which is being played. The performer plays it by means of a wire plectrums (mizrabs) worn on the fingers of the right hand, which pluck the strings near the bridge. The notes are stepped with a piece of roundd glass, rather like a paper weight.

(i)   Rabab

Rabab is made from wood. It has a double belly, the first being concerned with parchment & the second with wood. There are four strings; the upper two are some times doubled in which case the instrument has 6 strings. A number of sympathetic strings of metal run beneath the main strings. The instrument has 4 to 5 frets made up of gut tied round the finger board at semitonic intervals and the instrument is played with plectrum.

The instrument is popular in the Middle East as well. However, the Indian rabab is principally played in Kashmir, Punjab and Afghanisthan. It is popularly believed that Tansen of Akbar's court used to play a kind of rabab. His deciples were divided into two groups, namely the beenkars and the rababi yas. Among the great masters, Pyar Khan, Bahadur Khan and Bahadur Sain were noted rababiyas.

(j) **Gottu Vadyam**

This instrument is one of the important concert instrument of South India. It is similar to Southern Veena, the main difference being that unlike Veena, it has no frets. Gottuadyam consists of 6 main strings, which pass over the bridge placed on the top of the bowl. There are 3 side strings for the drone and rhythmic effect. The instrument is also provided with a few symphathetic strings which pass over a small bridge beneath the main bridge.

The musician plays the music by moving a cylindircal piece of heavy polished wood or horn over the strings. The instrument has a range of 4 to 4 1/2 octaves. Raga alapana, tanam plallavi and all other musical forms that are possible on the Veena can be played on Gottu Vadyam.

This instrument is believed to have been in vogue in South India for 80-90 years. It was brought by the famous musician Sakharam Rao of Tiruvidaimarudur, a village on the banks of Kaveri (Krishna Murthy 1965 : 33)

(k) **Sarangi**

In Indian classical music, Sarangi takes a prominent place as an accompaniment to the main artist in Vocal concerts in North. This instrument according to Krishna Murthy is said to be closest to human voice.

Sarangi is two feet long. It is prepared by hollowing out a single block of wood and covering it with parchment. A bridge is placed on the belly in the middle. The sides of this instrument are pinched to facilitate bowing. The instrument usually has 3 main strings of gut, varying thickness. Rarely, a fourth string made up of brass is used for drone.

A musician plays Sarangi by placing it on the lap vertically. Its head rests on the shoulders of the performer and is played with a horse hair bow, which is held in the right hand. The fingers of the left hand are used for stopping the strings. While this is being done the finger board as in the case of violin but press against the strings at the sids. Modern Sarangis generally have thirty five to forty sympathetic strings running under the main strings.

(l)	**Dilruba**	

Dilruba is a clever combination of Sitar and Sarangi, because its finger board and frets very much resemble with Sitar, while the belly of the instrument, which is covered with skin like a Sarangi and is played with a bow.

The stem of the instrument contains 18 to 19 eliptical frets which are movable. They are tied to frets and can be moved according to the scale of the raga, which is being played. The bridge is placed on the skin covered body, over which all the main sympathetic strings pass. Of the four man strings the last string is the principal playing string. Out of these four strings, the first two are made up of brass while the last two are of steel. There are 22 sympathetic strings or tarabs running underneath the frets and are festened to a series of pegs on the side. Like similar sympathetic strings in other instruments, the rarabs are tuned to reproduce the sclae of the melody which is being played.

Bowing of the instrument is done with right hand, while the fingers of the left hand are used to play over the strings. The frets on the Dilruba are meant only to guide the player in locating the correct position of the notes. The fingers do not pull the strings over the frets literally as in Sitar, but more longitudinally along the strings.

The performer holds the instrument vertically, the lower portion is kept on the lap, in front of him & the top rests against his left shoulder.

(m)	**Mandar Bahar**	

The Mandar Bahar is a similar instrument to Esraj in construction, but the finger board and the body are bigger in size, being about 4 feet long. Thick strings of gut are used to give deep, rich tone some what like the Western Violin cello.

To play the instrument, the performer sits on a low stool, places the instrument in front of him with the top placed on his left shoulder.

(n)   Esraj

The Esraj belongs to the family of Dilruba. It is very similar to the Dilruba in appearnace and in the technique of playing. However, there are few structural differences.

The body of Dilruba is rectangular and flat like that of the Sarangi, whereas the body of Esraj is round in shape and shallower in the middle The stem or the finger board of Dilruba is larger than the Esraj, hence the tone of the Dilruba is more rich and resonant than that of Esraj, whose tone is soft & mellow.

(o)   Santoor

In appearance the instrument is rectangular box over which strings of varying length are stretched. The long side of the rectangle faces the performer and the string run parallel to the longer side. The Santoor has a set of 3 strings to a note. The length and the thickness vary according to the octove. A Santoor player strikes the strings to produce melody.

(p)   Swarmandal

A Swarmandal is a rectangular box over which strings of varying length & pitch are stretched. This instrument is used mostly by vocalists, while singing. It is also used as an accompaniment instrument

The performer plucks the strings with his fingers, to produce melodious sounds.

(q)   Tun Tuna or Ektara

As the name suggests, it is string instrument which has one stirng tied to a stick or stem's top and is stretched in such a way that its other side is tied at the bottom of a tin or wooden vessel. This instrument is played in the temples and accompanies, Bhajan & folk singers.

3.4 Vitata or Rhythm Instruments :

Some of the major rhythm instruments in Indian classical music are :

(a) Pakhawaj

(b) Mrindaga

(c) Tabla

(d) Khanjeri

(e) Tavil

(f)   Ghatam

(g)   Damaru

(h)   Khol

(i)   Manjira

(j)   Taal

(k)   Dholak

(l)   Dholaki

(m) Nagara

(n)   Chenda

(o)   Shudda Maddalam

(p)   Dhol

(q)   Urmi

(r)   Huruk

(s)   Tumbaknari

(t)   Duff

(u)   Udukku

(v)   Chimta

Table number 3.2 gives description of rhythm instruments which are popular in Indian classical music.

Table No. 3.2

Brief Description of Rhythm Instruments

S. No.	Instrument	Brief Description
(a)	Pakhawaj	The Pakhawaj also called mridang belongs to the North and is also similar to mridangam of the South except for slight differences in construction and technique of playing. The left side is more or less the same in both the regions, but the right side though designed on the same principles, isquite different in the distribution of parts. There is difference in style of playing as well. The left side of pakhawaj is playe with open left hand.
		It is used to accompany Rudra Veena, Sur Shringar and the Surbahar. This instrument was very popular during the Moghul rule.
(b)	**Mrindaga**	This rhythm instrument is very popular in South India. It is hollowed out of a block of wood, and is cy-

lindrical in shape. It is one and a half to two feet long. Skin covers are stretched tight over both openings and are fastened to leather by hoops held tight by leather braces which pass along the length of the mridangam.

In between the braces & the wall of the instruments are wedged round blocks of wood which can alter pitch of the instrument it pushed up or down. Usually a mixture of flour and water is worked on to the middle of the left side of lower the tone to the desired pitch. This kind of plaster adds to the resonance & gives a full brass sound.

In the South, Mridangam is used as an instrument of accompaniment, but in every recital of classical music vocal or instrumental, there is short solo piece of mridangam.

(c)   Tabla

Tabla is an invention of Amir Khusro, who flourished in the reign of Alauddin Khilji during 13th century. It consists of two drums, one played with right hand, while the second played with left hand. The small one (Madhi) is usually hollowed out of a block of wood, where as the bigger one (Dagga) is either made up of clay, steel or copper.

Both the drums are coverd with skin fasten to leather hoops, which are stretched over the drums by means of leather braces. The Tabla has highly developed technique of playing and in the hands of a master it is capable of producing almost all the patterns of rhythm that a musician can conceive of.

The well established cycles (talas) are rendered in terms of drumming phrases (bols) called Theka. Theka constitutes the drummer's, basic structure which he elaborates and upon which he freely improvises.

(d)   Khanjeri

Khanjeri is one of the most ancient rhythm instrument of the percussion variety. It consists of a circular wooden frame about ten inches in diameter and two and a half inches board. Across one side, some type of skin preferably that of the wild lizard is stretched. The other side is open.

The frame is provided with three or four slits and a few pieces of metal or coins and inserted in a crossbar inside the slit. These make a jingling sound when the instrument is shaken.

The instrument is usually held in the left hand and the palm and fingers of the right hand are used to strike the skin to produce sound. It is used all over India for accompanying folk songs, and devotional music.

(e)	Tavil	This instrument consists of a barrel shaped shell hollowed out of a solid block of wood. The skins on the two sides of the instrument are stretched over hoops made of hamp and six or seven bamboo stick bundled together. The hoops are fastened to the shell by means of inter laced leather throngs.

The right side of the instrument is played with right hand, wrist and fingers, while the left side is played with a stout stick.

(f)   Ghatam

Ghatam is only an earthern pot with a narrow mouth and a big bely. It is naturally one of the most ancient percussion instruments in existence. In north India it is called Ghata and is extensively used to accompany folk music. Where as in the South Ghatam finds a place of honour in the most classical music concerts. It is played with two hands, the wrists, ten fingers and nails. Pazhani Krishna Iyer was a great exponent of Ghatam in recent memory.

(g)   Damaru

A damaru is a small drum. It is also known as dhaka in Sanskrit. Damaru is an attribute of Lord Shiva, who is said to have played it during the cosmic dance. This is evident in ancient sculptures.

The length of a damaru, varies from six inches to one foot. A small ball of metal cork is attached over the braces connecting the two heads. The heads are covered with parchment. The instrument is held in the right hand and rolled from side to side. As the drum shakes, the end of the string bearing the metal balls strike the centre of both heads alternately and produces rhythmical strokes. This instrument is popular among the snake charmers, madaris, jugglers and wandering minstrels in India.

(h)   Khol

This instrument is made up of burnt clay closely covered with thin strips of leather than the left side and is two or three inches in diameter. The pitch is constant and cannot be altered as in other drums. It is a popular accompaniment rhythm instrument in devotional music.

(i)	Manjira	Manjira is a pair of small metalic cymbals used for rhythmic purposes. They are flat, circular discs, usually connected by a cord, passing through a hole in their centres. This instrument is an accompaniment rhythm instrument in devotional music.
(j)	Taal	Taal is also pair of small metalic cymbals, which resemble with manjira. The difference being in the size. Taal is little larger in size than the manjiras.
(k)	Dholak	This instrument is a very popular in Indian orchestras. It is a circular drum with skin on both the ends played by wrists and fingers.
(l)	Dholaki	Dholaki is a longish circular drum popularly played in North India. In Maharashtra it was played in tamashas (traditional dramas and dances). The right circular end has a skin cover which sounds on a higher pitch, while the left side circular end gives base rhythm.
(m)	Nagara	The nagara is also called naggara and is one of the oldest percussion instruments in existence. It is a big conical drum covered with hide. Most temples and religious institutions in India own one. There are Nagaras with a diameter of five feet. A set of nagaras usually accompanies shehanai players in the North. One drum is smaller than the other and are played with sticks.
(n)	Chenda	This is a cylindrical wooden drum, two feet in length and about a foot in diameter, both sides are coverd with skin. The drum hangs in front of the player who beats it while standing, with two sticks held in both hands.
		In a Kathakali dance recital the chenda is generally played along with maddalam, a drum similar to Northern pakhawaj.
(o)	Shudda Maddalam	This rhthm instrument is based on the same principle as the ordinary Mridangam except that it is bigger in size and has a different style of playing.
(p)	Dhol	The Dhol is one of the commonest percussion instruments in India, mainly used for accompanying folk

music. It adds to give a gay air to festivals and ceremonial ocassions.

It is a barrel-shaped drum, made up of wood, usually 18 to 20 inches in length & 12 inches in diameter. The skin on both heads is stretched round the leatherhoops.

(q)	Urmi	Urmi is a double sided drum, which is narrow in the centre and broadens towards ends. It is longer than pambai (another south Indian drum). This drum is played with a curved stick about one and a half feet long, which is held in the left hand The stick is rubbed against the skinned surface on the left side producing a sound resembling the growling of an animal Urmi is mainly used for funeral procession and never for celebration or auspicious functions.
(r)	Huruk	The huruk is built on the principle of the damaru, but it is bigger in size. Both ends are covered with skin and laced with cotton thread. The instrument is hung over the left shoulder and the right side of the drum is beaten with hands. The left hand holds the central braces and varies the tension, thereby effecting changes in the tone of the same. It is popular instrument for accompanying folk songs in the hilly districts of Garhwal, Kumaon in Uttar Pradesh.
(s)	Tumbaknari	Tumbaknari is a drum used by the people of Kashmir. It is shaped like a long neck water pot with bottem knocked of and covered with skin. The instrument is held under the arm and played with right hand. This instrument is popular for accompany folk songs.
(t)	Duff	The duff is an open circular frame, with only one side covered with skin. It can be played either with hand or with sticks. These drums are used usually to accompany music, devotional songs, and dance of the common folk.
(u)	Udukku	The udukku or udukkai is a small drum, about one foot in length, with a narrow waste in the middle. Its two sides are covered with thin membrane and laced with cotton twine. The main body of the instrument is made up of brass, wood or clay. it is held in the left hand and played upon by the fingers of the right hand. It is an important accompaniment to the Kathakali dance - drama.

| (v) | Chimta | The chimta is a rhythmic instrument popular in Punjab and neighbouring region It consists of two flat metal pieces with pointed ends. One end is however joined together by an iron ring. The instrument is held in both the hands and pressed to give rhythmic effects. |

Well, there are several rhythm or ghana instruments, played all over India. We have not included tribal rhythm instrument in the above list, as the focus of the book may take a different turn. However, for a lay person, who is new to Indian classical music, we thought it was necessary for him to have a background of these instruments and the history of the musical traditions too.

The next section in Chapter three throws light on some of the major wind or sushir instruments in Indian classical music.

3.5 Sushir or Wind Instruments :

If one goes across the length and breadth of India, he may find several types of wind instruments. We are however presenting the most popular sushir or wind instruments used in Indian classical music. These are :

(a)   Shahnai

(b)   Flute

(c)   Clarenet

(d)   Alghoza

(e)   Harmonium

(f)   Organ

Table No. 3.3

Brief. Description of Wind Instruments

S. No.	Instrument	Brief Description
(a)	Shahnai	This double-reeded instrument belongs to the sushira (wind) category are among the most ancient and most widely-known musical instruments in the world. Shahnai is a tube that gradually widens towards the lower end. It usually has eight to nine holes, the upper seven are used for playing. The remaining are either stopped with wax or kept open. This is left to the discretion of the performer since the purpose is to regulate the pitch of the instrument.
		Shahnai is made up of dark closed grouned black wood and has a metal bell fixed to the broader end. The length of the instrument is one and a half to two feet. The reed is fixed at the narrow blowing end. The

playing of shahnai is a very complicated technique.

(b)   Flute

Flute, a wind musical instrument is known by various names such a bansuri, venu, vamshi, kuzhal, murali and so on. It is one of the most ancient wind instruments. References of flute an found in Indian Sculptures from the beginning of the 1st century B. C., at Sanchi and later or in Greco-Buddhist plastic art at Gandharva.

Flute is a simple cylindrical tube, mostly made up of bamboo of uniform bore, closed at one end. Their are different kinds of flutes and their number of holes vary.

The instrument is held in a horizontal position with a slight downward indication, where the two thumbs are used to hold the flute in position, the three fingers of the left hand, excluding the little finger, and the four of the right hand are used to manipualte the finger holes.

(c)   Clarenet

The clarenet is a wind instrument, popular in the West. Like the violin, clarenet has been used by number of Indian performers to play Hindustani classical Ragas on it. As regards the description of clarenet, it does not require description of clarenet, it does not require description as it is popular instrument played in orchestras and musical bands.

(d)   Alghoza

The Alghoza is a ordinary flute, with four finger holes ad is played by blowing straight through the mouth hole. Usually Alghoza is played in pairs by the same person and the effect produced is most enchanting.

(e)   Harmonium

Harmonium is the most popular wind (sushir) instrument, widely used by classical vocalists, ghazal and folk singers in India. The instrument has key board like that of the casio, except it works on bellows manually. Harmonium is the most melodious musical instrument of the sushir category. The harmonium was invented by D. Bain in the year 1540.

Given this background, of some of the popular string, rhythm, wind and side rhythm instruments of Indian classical music, let us unravel the place of Rudra Veena in Indian Classical Music.

❏ ❏ ❏

4

Place of Rudra Veena, In Indian Classical Music

4.1. History and Ancient glory of the instrument

Rudra Veena is the mother of all stringed instruments. In fact according to Hindu myth, Rudra -means Shanker or Shiva, the Greater of the universe hence, the instrument is associated with him. It in believed that shiva made the first Rudra Veena & used his own intestines as strings of the same. Even Ravana the demon - who was a devotee of lord Shiva, is believed to be a player of Rudra Veena & used it to, create devotional music so as to please shiva. there is a myth about Ravana, who was Playing Rudra Veena to please Shiva. Lord Shiva who was so engrossed with listening to the Sweet sound, was enjoying the Same. But, while Ravana was Playing it, one of the Strings broke, yet he Continued to play the remaining Strings, as he did not want Shiva to be disturbed. Interestingly Ravana replaced the broken string with his own nerve. This is how he respected Shiva by maintaining peaceful & happy atmosphere.

The Hindu literature also consider's Rudra Veena as an instrument played by gods & God deses in heaven. It is believed, that Shiva Passed on the art of music to Saraswati and Saraswati gave at to Narada & Hanumantha, who brought it on Earth. That is how man was able to learn the same. A variety of Veenas, drums, pipes, gongs and bells are shown is the ancient sculptures of Bharhut, Gandhara, Amaravati, Sandhi, Nagarjuna konda, konark, the temples of southern India and the frescoes and paintings of Ajantha, Bagh Tanjavoer etc. This is a true picture of the past.

4.2. Structure of Rudra Veena

The Rudra Veena consists of a bamboo fret board, about 26 inches long and two and half inches wide, upon which are fixed 24 metalic frets, one for each of four octaves. The fret is fixed on the stem, by a resinous wax like substance. This fret board is mounted on two large gourds, in about 54 inches in diameter.

The instrument has four main strings for playing, it also has the side string. The diagram given below depicts Rudra Veena and its parts.

Diagram 4.1

Rudra Veena and Its Parts.

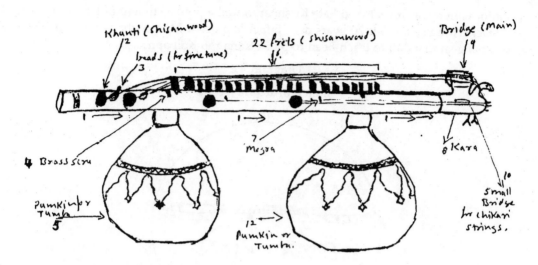

(1) Stem—also known as Dandi

(2) Pegs—also known as Khunti

(3) Beads—also known as Badak

(4) Brass—also known as pitali screw

(5) Pumpkin—also known as Bhopala or tumba.

(6) Frets—also known as Padade.

(7) Mogra—also known as Panja.

(8) Kara—also known as Kara only.

(9) Main Bridge—also known as Ghodi

(10) Small Bridge left side—also known as Davi Lahan ghodi

(11) Small Bridge Right side—also known as Lahan ghodi

(12) Pumpkin—also known as Bhopala, or tamba.

Regarding the Structure of Rudra-Veena, Late Ustad Murad Khan, the Guru of Late Krishnarao Kolhapure, revealed to that, Been's structure is based on the concept of a peacock's body. How the structure of Rudra-Veena corresponds with that of peacocks body can be well understood from the analogy given below.

(i) Dhandi or Bamboo Corresponds with the Central body of peacock.

(ii) The Kara or bridge made up of ivory peacock, which is on the right side, Corresponds with peacock's feathers.

(iii) The strings on the Bamboo & the Is its Corresponds with the stick like structures attached to every long feather of the Peacock.

(iv) The seven Strings on right, left & middle one pulses of The feathers.

This information was revealed to Late Krishnarao Kolha pure a student of late ustad murad khan (his teacher) himself about 70 years ago. Infact late ustad Murad khan was requested by the Balwant Sangeet mandali to teach Been to pt. Krishna rao Kolhapure.

Diagram 4.2

Sketch of Rudra Veena

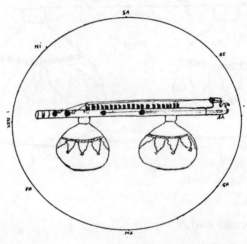

(4.3) How to Tune Rudra Veena.

Rudra Veena has seven Strings in all, and each String produces a note or swar. The sequence of the same is given in table No 4.1.

Table No 4.1.
Sequence of Rudra Veena Strings

S. No.	String Sequence	Note or Swar	Western Chord
(1)	Side strings Chikari string	Sa (Kali -2) Madhya Saptak	D Sharp (Middle Scale)
(2)	Chikari string	Sa (Kali 2) (Tar Saptak).	D Sharp (Higher Scale)
	Main Strings in the centre		
(3)	Baj String or first string in the centre	Ma (Madhya saptak)	F Chord (middle Scale)

(4)	Second string	Sa (Mandra Saptak)	D Sharp (Lower Scale)
(5)	Third String	Pa (Mandra Saptak)	G (Lower Scale)
(6)	Fourth String	Sa (Ati Mandra Saptak)	D Sharp (Lower Scale)
(7)	Side String	Sa (Kali 2) or	D Sharp (Lower Scale).
	(Tambora String)	Mandra Saptak	

Given the background of the structure and styles of Rubra Veena. Let us now take lessons of Rudra - Veena in ten Raghas namely

1. Yaman Ragh -

2. Bhup Ragh -

3. Brindavan Sarang Ragh -

4. Bhageshree Ragh -

5. Bihag Ragh -

6. Mal Kaunse Ragh -

7. Puriya Kalyan Ragh -

8. Darbari Kannada Ragh -

9. Miya Malhar Ragh -

10. Bhairavi Ragh -

These lesson are given in the appendix section of this book.

(4.4) Masters of Sound and Silence

This section of chapter four presents an account of the famous Beenkars (Rudra Veena players), of India. Although, Rudra Veena in an ancient instrument, and that its origin is linked with shiva, there is not much information about Rudra Veena per formers from pre-vedic & Vedic times. However, records & references of Rudra Veena Players or Beenkars are available Since the reign of Mughals in India.

Data collected by the authors of this book, from the elderly Beenkars in India, reveals that, most of them can trace back the history of Rudra from Vena players from Ustad Bande Ali khan (Beenkar). Ustad Bande Ali khan was originally from North India & his birth date revealed in literature is some where in 1830. He died in Pune & his grave is under the new bridge apposite Shaniwar wada. Bande Ali khan was known for Playing dhrupad baj and Khayalia baj on the Rudra Veena. Out of many, of his desciples two were popular, namely ustad Murad khan and Ustad Rajab Ali khan. The Speciality of Ustad Murad khan & Ustad Rajab Ali khan was that, besides being Beenkars, they were great singers as well.

The flow chart No 4.2 given below directs some famous Rudra Veena players & theirs desciples, starting from ustad Bande Ali khan's time.

Flow chart No. 4.2
Rudra Veena players from 1855 to date Ustad Bande Ali Khan
(Beenkar)

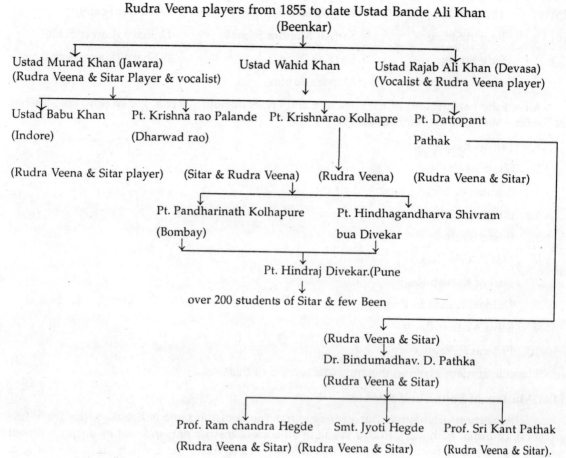

From the above flow chart a brief account of the Beenkars & their efforts to preserve and popularize Rudra Veena is given below.

(1) Late Ustad Bande Ali Khan (1830 to 27th July, 1895)

The Beenkars of Pune always pay homage to Late Ustad Bande Ali Khan on Guru Pornima, by offering an incense stick, flowers or at least touch grave. This ritual is done to seek the blessing of Late Ustad Bande Ali Khan. Ustad Bande Ali Khan hailed from North India, born in 1830. He belonged to the musician gharana of Hasan Khan. An admirer and a lover of music. Khan Sahib took interest in learning Been & mastered it. He got married to the daughter of Late Haddukhan a famous vocalist during Mughal rule.

Ustad Bande Ali Khan was very popular Been player during his time. Being a court musician in Indore, he also performed in most royal courts of North India. He even gave Rudra Veena lessons to the son of Maharaja of Gwalior, Shri Balwantrao Bhaiya. He also performed concerts in North India.

Later he took on to teaching Rudra Veena to his students. Some of his noted students are pandit Bhaskarbuva Bakhala, Ustad Wahid Khan, Ustad Rajab Ali Khan and others. Once he played Been in the court of Smt. Jeyajirao of Gwalior, who was so pleased with his performance, that he asked Ustad Bande Ali Khan, what does he want from the Maharaja. Khan Sahiib replied, I want you to give me "Chunna Bai" — a famous vocalist. Everyone was surprised by this demand, though. The king asked Chunna Bai, whether she was interested in going with Bande Ali Khan, who was very elder to her. (Sawant Sulekh 1984: 5)

Chunna Bai did agree to go with Bande Ali Khan. The main intention of taking Chunna Bai was to teach her the art of playing Rudra Veena. Being a vocalist, Chunna Bai did have a sound background in classical music. She mastered the art of playing of Rudra Veena, as she took lessons from the Maestro. She also moved with him from place to place.

An incident narrated by Nata Sretha Chintoba Gurav (Divekar), who lived during Bande Ali Khan's time, depicts, how much support Chunnabai gave Bande Ali Khan, as a pupil.

Ustad Bande Ali Khan was once summoned to give a concert in Pune. Late Chintoba Guruv attended this programme then. While the programme was going on , Khan Sahib, had a cough attack, which made him stop playing the instrument. This hindered the mood of the audience. However, Chunnabai who was there, immediately went upto him, she tore a part of her new Sari (Called Shalu) and also gave him a glass of water. This helped him to get back to his normal health. After this, he began playing the Been melodiously. This shows her devotion to Ustad Bande Ali Khan as his student, and his wife too.

The great Maestro of Been, breathed his last in Pune, on 27th July, 1895. His grave still exists on the bank of the river, under the new bridge opposite Shaniwar Wada Fort.

(2) Late Chunna Bai

As mentioned earlier, Bande Ali Khan developed liking for Chunna Bai, a famous singer, who was given to Bande Ali Khan by Jeeyaji Maharaj after consulting her. Although Bande Ali Khan was very old compared to Chunnabai, yet she chose to go with him, as she was a great lover of music. Khan Sahib, no doubt took her as his student and taught her the art of playing Been.

Infact, Chunnabai is perhaps the first known woman Beenkar as per literature, in the history of Rudra Veena. She accompanied Bande Ali Khan, whenever, he went. He was the chief musician at the court of Shivajirao Maharaj of Indore. After the death of Shivajirao Maharaj , Ustad Ali Khan & Chunna bai moved to Hydrabad. When, Khan Saheb died in Pune on 27th July, 1895, Chunnabai left for Dharampur, where she settled & four to five years, after that i.e. during (1899-1900), she died in Barhanpur. Not much is known about her concerts as a Beenkar, and also about her, imparting training to women students, especially.

We certainly respect and honour this great vocalist and female Beenkar, who lived to promote, preserve and propagate Rudra Veena, especially during the reign of Britishers when India was not independent. Her name certainly will shine in the History of Indian classical music.

(3) Late Ustad Murad Khan

Ustad Murad Khan hailed from Jawara. His father Ustad Maglu Khan was very famous sitar player and belonged to the then famous Amritsen sitar Gharana. Murad Khan's father Maglu Khan once attended the concert of Ustad Bande Ali Khan and was so much impressed that, he asked his son to take lessons from Bande Ali Khan.

As desired by his father, Murad Khan, went to Bande Ali Khan and started serving him. For almost one year he was not given any lesson in Rudra Veena by his teacher. He therefore got frustrated & came back to his father's house, and complained that he was not given any training for one full year. On hearing this, Murad Khan's father fired him & send him back to his teacher. Well, Murad Khan did go back to his Guru, where he received lessons of Rudra Veena. He mastered the art & became famous during his time. He popularized Rudra Veena in North & Central India. He also performed in Karnataka. While at Karnataka he would live with Mr. Shamnath Babu Gurty-a music lover, from Dharwad.

In the year 1913, Ustad Murad Khan, worked for the Balwant Sangeet Mandali — a drama company started by Master Dinanath Mangeshkar. He also asked him to teach Been (Rudra Veena) to Pt. Krishnarao Kolhapure.

In Pune his programme was organized by Late Mrs. Yallubai Mane, at her house in Shukruwar Peth. During that time, she paid Murad Khan Rs. 100/- per day as an honorarium. This was in the year 1920. This programme was attended by Shri Chintoba Divekar & Pt. Shivrambuva Divekar (grandfather & father of Pt. Hindraj Divekar).

In the year 1927, Murad Khan went to Bombay, wherein he was received by Prof. B.R. Deodhar, on the advice of Dr. Babasaheb Bhajekar. Prof. B.R. Deodhar organized 8-9 programmes of Ustad Murad Khan. In 1928, Ustad Murad Khan played for All India Radio, in Bombay. This was perhaps the first time in the history of Rudra Veena, that its sound was broad casted on air (Deodhar B.R. 1952:14).

Initially, Ustad Murad Khan did not like the idea of playing alone, without any audience. Finally Prof. Deodhar had to get 15 to 20 people in the studio so as to motivate Murad Khan to play. Murad Khan than demanded, that he wanted to listen how he played the Been. Well, this was the reaction of earlier Beenkar's, who were so traditional.

Prof. Deodhar who had a music school, requested Nirsar Hussain, Murad Khan's son to teach in his school. However, after few months Nisar had to go back to Jawara state, with his family. After reaching Jawara, few days later Nisar died. This was a shock to Murad Khan.

He taught many students the art of playing Rudra Veena. Some of his prominent students were Babu Khan (Indore), Musrat Khan (Ahemadabad), Krishanrao Kolhapure (Bombay), Pt. Dattopant Pathak (Dharwad) and Krishanrao palande (Dharwad).

(4) Late Ustad Rajab Ali Khan (1875-1959)

Ustad Rajab Ali Khan was a resident of Devas. He was born in 1875. His father Mugool Khan was a well wisher of music and more importantly Rudra Veena. He therefore send his son Rajab Ali Khan to Ustad Bande Ali Khan for training.

Thus, at an early age of 15, Rajab Ali went to learn Been from his Guru Bande Ali Khan, in Indore. Those days, Bande Ali Khan was the chief musician at the court of Shivajirao Maharaj.

Along with Rajab Ali, Ustad Murad Khan & Najju Khan were also learning Been. After his education he became very famous.

Infect Ustad Rajab Ali Khan was called by Balasaheb Gaikwad to Kolhapur in South Maharashtra. He and his father lived in Kolhapur. It is said that Ustad Rajab Ali Khan also played in the court of Shahu Maharaj of Kolhapur. He lived in Kolhapur from 1895 to 1915.

In these years he trained many students. He was honoured by the president of India, at the Sangeet Natak Academy, New Delhi. No gramophone record of Ustad Rajab Ali Khan is available, however, the sangeet Natak Academy, New Delhi had audio tapes, Ustad Rajab Ali Khan's Been. After his great service to Indian classical music and more precisely his efforts to presence the art of playing Rudra Veena for almost 74 years of his life, Khan Sahib breathed his last in Devas on 8th January, 1959. Prominent among his students are pandit Dattopant Pathak or Dharwad in Karnataka state, of southern India.

(5) Late Pt. Krishnarao Kolhapure

Late Pt. Krishnarao Kolhapure is one of the giants in the history of famous Beenkars. He was born in Bombay. He received his training in Rudra Veena from Ustad Murad Khan student of Late Bande Ali Khan.

Late Ustad Murad Khan was requested by Master Dinanath Mangeshkar to be a part of the Balwant Sangeet Mandali, owned by Dinanath Mangehkar, Pt. Krishnarao Kolhapure & Shri Kolhatkar. Pt. Krishnarao Kolhapure was asked to learn Been from Ustad Murad Khan. Ustad certainly did justice to Pt. Kolhapure. He taught Kolhapure both Dhrupad baj & Khyali baj. As a Rudra Veena artist, Pt. Kolhapure certainly proved to be a great Beenkar of his time. His other colleague Beenkars and also students of Ustad Murad Khan are Ustad Babu Khan from Indore, Pt. Krishnarao Palande from Dharwad, and Pt. Datto pant Pathak of Hubli.

Besides being a Beenkar, Pt. Krishnarao Kolhapure was a great actor and a vocalist as well. He became very popular through, the Balwant sangeet Mandali. Later on the drama company had to be closed. He then moved to Baroda in Gujarat, wherein he worked as a Beenkar for the Baroda Sansthan. His main aim there was to popularize Been & teach more and more students. He rendered Been concerts in Gujarat, Madhyapradesh, Maharashtra and other parts of India. Out of the many students of Pt. Krishnarao Kolhapur prominent among them are his own son pt. pandharinath Kolhapure, the father of famous Hindi film actress, Padmini Kolhapure, and Pt. Hindgandharva Shivrambuva Divekar, the father of Pt. Hindraj Divekar.

Thus, after dedicating his entire life for the preservation, promotion and popularization of Marathi drama, singing and playing Rudra Veena, the great maestro breathed his last on June 11, 1953, to bid a good bye to the world of music and drama.

(6) Late Pt. Krishnarao Palande (Dharwad)

Yet another famous Beenkar and student of Late Ustad Murad Khan, is Pt. Krishna Rao Palande from Dharwad district of Karnataka state. The credit to preserve Rudra Veena & propagate it in karnataka to krishnarao Palande.

(7) Late Ustad Abdul Karim Khan

Ustad Abdul Karim Khan was not only a famous Been player but a singer as well. He was born in 1872. He did contribute to the preservation, promotion & propagation of Rudra Veena. As a player of Been he performed several concerts in the courts & theatres. On 27th October,

1937, he died in Miraj — a town in Southern Maharashtra. He was known for playing the Khyaliya baj style on the Been.

(8) Ustad Asad Ali Khan

Ustad Asad Ali Khan a disciple of his father. He played Rudra Veena or Been from Dhrupad baj style. He is from Delhi. He performed not only in India, but abroad as well. He would play Rudra Veena accompanied by pakhawaj an ancient drum. He has also rendered concerts & programmes for radio concerts & abroad, yet another worthy son of the Been, ustad Asad Ali Khan contributed to preservation of this antique ancient instrument called Rudra Veena.

(9) Late Ustad Ziyamoiuddin Dagar

Ustad Ziyamoiuddin Dagar was a world famous Rudra Veena player of his time. Born in the family of a musician, Dagar received training in Rudra Veena from his father Ziyauddin Dagar. His father used to play Been in the courts of Udaipur, in Rajasthan.

Ustad Ziyamoiddin Dagar rendered Rudra-Veena performances both in India & abroad. He also performed for All India Radio & Doordarshan. He has toured in Europe & America to render Been concerts. Some of his students abroad are philip Brugier, Monica Lokombe & Dr. Kim Wardroof. In India Dr. R. Sanyal, Ashish Banerjee, Chandrashekhar Nargekar etc. are prominent disciples of Shri Dagar.

In his article which appeared in sakal a Marathi news paper on May, 15th, 1986, Ashok Ranade, points out the changes made by Ustad Ziyamoiuddin Dagar in the structure of Been. The Ustad himself reported that, earlier there were seven string, he added one more & made eight strings. He was also responsible to increase the size of 'Paradas' (frets) from two & quarter inches to three and a half inches.

He also said that the detachability of gourds was his idea. However, the Rudra-Veena possessed by Pt. Hindraj Divekar has one hundred years old and has detachable gourds. His father Pt. Hindagandharva Shivram Divekar had purchased it from a Muslim Beenkar in the year 1930. The muslim Beenkar revealed that he had bought the Been forty years ago. His contribution to the Indian classical music will be remembered for ages.

(10) Late Pandit G.B. Acharekar

Pt. Acharekar *is* known as a Khyaliya Beenkar. He was born in Achare village in the year 1885. He learnt the art of singing and music under the able guidance of Late Balkrishna and Pt. Balwant Bapat. He worked sincerely and honestly to master the art of music and singing. During the years 1910 to 1939, Pt. Acharekar was very famous. He also worked in the Saurashtra Rajkumar college. He taught Pt. Shivram Divekar Been & singing. This great artist, died in the year 1939, in Bombay.

(11) Late Pandit Hindhagandharva, Shivram Buva Divekar

Pandit Hindgandharva Shivrambuva Divekar was born on April, 1, 1912, in Purandar block of Pune district, in the state of Maharashtra. As a child he received lessons in music, acting & singing from his father, Late Natsrestha clintoba Divekar and subsequently from well known artists such as late G.B. Archarekar, Bhaiyasaheb Ashtewale, late Ustad Inayatkhan (Tandraksha Gharane) & late master Dinanath Mangeshkar. He received his education in Rudra Veena (Been) from late Pt. Krishna rao Kolhapure.

Thus Pt. Shivaram Divekar has been brought up under the guidance of a great son of Marathi theatre. Pandit Shivrambuva worked as an actor, singer and even director (teleem Master) for the drama companies mentioned above. In the year 1938, he was selected as lecturer of music in Government Training college, Pune, where he succeeded famous G.B. Acharekar. He learnt music and singing and later on composed music & songs for All India Radio as well.

As a professor of music, he made sincere efforts to study & understand musical instruments like Been, Sitar, Dilruba, Nalika, Tarang, Jaltarang, Kashta tarang, Tabla, Harmonium, Organ & so on.

Some of his famous dramas were:-

(i)   Lagnachi Bedhi;

(ii)   Bramhacha Bhopala;

(iii) Sangeet Sharda;

(iv)   Sanshaya Kallol;

(v)   Usna Navara;

(vi)   Chameyee Chama etc.

As a famous Rudra Veena player of his time, he rendered several concerts. He thought Been to several students. Prominent among them were his son Hindraj Divekar, who also plays sitar.

Late Pandit Shivrambuva, hails from the Beenkar tradition of late Bande Ali Khan, Gharana. He also contributed in establishing the Arya sangeet prasasak Mandali, as a Founder member. This organization has been holding the Sawai Gandharva festival in Pune for over forty years. Panditji established his own organization called sangeet Maifil Mahavidyalaya in 1978.

Pt. Hindagandharva Shivam buva Divekar, performed in the court of the king of Mysore in South India. He along with his father had been to Mysore. His father was paid Rs. 300/- while, Pt. Shivrambuva was paid Rs. 100/- per day by the Maharaja those days. Besides rendering concerts in Mysore court, Panditji played Been in the court of Indore, Kolhapur of Shahu Maharaj, Devas, Miraj & Baroda.

The title of Hindgandharva was conferred on him by late Nyayaratna Dhondiraj Shastri vinod. The late Prime Minister of India, Shri Morarji Desai honoured Pt. Shivrambua Divekar, in Balgandharva Rangmandir, Pune. This programme was organized by Akhil Bhartiya Marathi Natya Sammelan, Pune. He thus, contributed to the development of music, Been, singing and acting.

Pt. Shivrambuva breathed his last, on 26th September, 1988.

(12) Pandit Pandharinath Kolhapure

Born in a family of great actor, singer & Beenkar, Pt. Krishnarao Kolhapure, Pt. Pandharinath grew up in an artistic environment. He received his education as a singer and Beenkar, from his father Late Pandit Krishnarao Kolhapure, a student of Late Ustad Murad Khan.

Besides learning Been & singing from his father, Pt. Pandharinath Kolhapure also learned music and singing from Late Pt. Madhusudan Joshi of Baroda (belonging to Agra gharana), Late professor B.R. Deodhar, and famous singer Late Pt. Kumar Gandharva. He has rendered programmes of Been & singing in well known musical festivals in Calcutta, Allahabad, Kanpur, Bombay, Delhi etc. He has been guiding and teaching Pt. Hindraj Divekar since 1988.

(13) Pandit Hindraj Divekar

(Dec. 4th 1954 --------)

Pandit Hinaraj Divekar, an international Musician of Rudra Veena & Sitar, is the only artist in India, who gives concerts of both Rudra Veena & Sitar, is known as the "Master of sound & silence". He has been declared as the magician of Rudra Veena by the Madhyapradesh Govt. Sanskriti Vibhag; Ustad Allauddin Khan Sansed Sameeti, Bhopal (M.P).

He has to his credit several titles in music. These are as follows :-

(i) Surmani:- Conferred on him by the Sur singer sansad, in 1980 for both sitar & Rudra Veena.

(ii) Sangeet Vadan Kala visharad:- by the Bharat Gayan Samaj Institute, Pune.

(iii) Pandit:- at the Varanasi music sammelan, in November, 1988.

(iv) Dhrupad Shree:- at the Pawar Bandhu Dhrupad sammelan in Indore, M.P, in 1994.

(v) Sangeet Shree:- at the Allahabad Music Sammelan, in 1988.

(vi) Hindgandharva Shree:- at the Hindgandharva sangeet Mahotsav, in 1989.

(vii) Been Bhaskar:- at the pawer Bandhu Dhrupad Sammelan Indore, Madhyapradesh in 1991.

(viii)Pune Gaurav' 94:- conferred on him, by the Mayor, of Pune Municipal corporation Pune, on 15th August, 1994.

Pandit Hindraj Divekar, alies Digambar Shivram Divekar was born on 4th December, 1954 -82 Budhawarpeth, in Pune. Brought up in a family of musicians, Hindraj was initiated into sitar and Rudra Veena playing by his father, Late Hindgandharva Pandit Shivrambuva Divekar (vocalist, Rudra veena player, and Marathi stage actor).

Hindraj's father was a disciple of Late Pt. Achrekar (Rudra veena player and a highly respected writer), Late Pt. Krishnarao Kolhapure (Rudra Veena player) Late Shankerbhaiya Ashtekar (Ujjain, M.P) and Late Pt. Master Dinanathji Mangeshkar (a great singer and marathi stage actor of India). Late Pt. Shivrambuva Divekar also belongs to tradition of the famous Beenkar of India, Late Ustad Bande Ali Khan.

Hindraj's grandfather, "Nat Sretha" Chintoba Gurav (Diekar), was an illustrious singer and a famous Marathi stage actor. Late Chintoba Gurav (Divekar) who was the only stage artist in the history of Indian drama, who has given continuous 65 years of dedicated service to Marathi theatre. Late Chintoba Gurav (Divekar) rendered several concerts & programmes in places like Kolhapur, ichalkaranji, Sangli, Miraj, Satara, Baroda, Indore, Dhar, Devas, Mysore etc. Pandit Hindraj's musical traditions of the family can therefore be traced back to at least seven generations.

Academic Qualifications

Besides his achievements in music, Pt. Hindraj Divekar has graduated in commerce & has a B.Com degree.

Teaching Experience In Academic Institutions

- Lecturer in the Department of Hindustani Music, spicaer memorial college, Pune-7.
- Founder Director:- Hindgandharva Sangeet Academy (Trust) 82 Budnawar Peth, Pune, 2, India.

Private Coaching

Pandit Hindraj has taught almost 200 students in India & abroad, both sitar & Rudra Veena. However, some of the prominent ones are:-

(i)   Dr. Horst Rolly from Germany;

(ii) Mitto From Switzerland;

(iii) Purana from Italy;

(iv) Gopal from U.S.A;

(v)   Ma Prem Daya from Germany;

(vi) Devakant from U.S.A.;

(vii) Manju from Japan;

(viii)Veeno from Switzerland;

(ix)Joshin Haim from Germany;

(x)Viren from England;

(xi)Nartana from Japan;

(xii) Gary from U.S.A.;

(xiii)Aseema from Italy;

(xiv)Mudita from Taiwan;

(xv) Gyan from Israel;

(xvi)Sharda Joshi from India;

(xvii)Dr. Jaison Gardosi from Australia;

(xix)Dr. Ian Duncan from Newzealand;

(xx) Morris from Australia;

(xxi)Alias Ekkerhard Grubler Germany;

(xxii)Rosario Iraeta from Spain;

(xxiii)Varsha Doshi from Malaysia;

(xxiv)Brigettee wagner from Germany;

(xxv)Guide Muller from Germany.

However, very few have taken to learning Rudra Veena.

Concerts Abroad

Besides the popular Sitar, Pt. Hindraj Divekar is an expert player of Rudra Veena. Rudra Veena which is a difficult string instrument of Indian classical music, is handled with brilliance by Hindraj. While the Sitar has came to be much popularized in India and abroad, the Rudra Veena has rarely been heard.

Pandit Hindraj Divekar is the first Rudra Veena player to play this instrument abroad. In the year 1979, he rendered the concert of Rudra Veena for the first time in Australia. Two of his Australian students Viren Sayer and Jaison, organized concerts in Australia. Table 4.3 gives details about the same.

Table No. 4.3

Concerts Rendered By Pt. Hindraj in Various Cities of Australia.

S.No.	City	Date	Day	Theatre/Hall
1.	Perth	22-04-1979	Sunday	Octagon Theatre.
2.	Adelaide	28-04-1979	Friday	Edmund Wright house.
3.	Adelaide	1-05-1979	Tuesday	Town Hall.
4.	Melbourne	4-05-1979	Friday	Dallas Brooks Hall.
5.	Sydney	6-05-1979	Friday	Town Hall.

Pt. Hindraj was interviewed at the Perth Airport by the ABCTV, Australia, and the press. He also played Rudra Veena for Australian Radio, at Perth.

(2) Concerts In Germany

Dr. Horst Rolly Organized concerts of Rudra Veena & Sitar in Germany in 1983. Pt. Hindraj rendered 22 concerts in major cities like Heidelberg, Frankfurt, Berlin, Mainz, Schesswig, Hamburg etc. He stated that playing in the Heidelberg castle for 1500 audience was an unique experience. He was interviewed for Radio & T.V, in Germany then.

(3) Concerts In Italy

Dr. Iris Schneller and Swami Sangeet, organized Rudra Veena & Sitar concerts of Pt. Hindraj in Italy, in the year 1989. He played in cities like Rome, Verize, Viena, Millano, Ferrara, Bologna, Floreng, Livorno and Viterbo. Pt. Hindraj was interviewed for Radio & T.V.

(4) Concerts In Singapore

In Singapore concerts were organized by Mr. Zunzunwala Lal Saheb from April to September, 1996.

(14)   Dr. Bindu Madhav D. Pathak

Dr. Bindu madhav D. Pathak a worthy son of a great Been (Rudra Veena) player, Pandit Datto Pant Pathak hails from Hubli. Born on 9th April, 1935, BinduMadhav Pathak was socialized in a musician's family. He obtained his early training in Rudra Veena and sitar from his father (pupil of late Ustad Murad Khan Beenkar of Jawara), and later from Ustad Rajab Ali Khan of Devas. Both Ustad Murad & Rajab Ali Khan were students of the great Rudra Veena player, Ustad Bande Ali Khan.

Dr. Bindu Madhav Pathak blossomed into an accomplished Artist at a very young age of seventeen. Today, he is among the foremost instrumentalist of India. Has a versatile career in Hindustani music as a Rudra Veena player of 'A' top grade. He has given Been recitals in the National Music Programmes, on All India Radio & ofcourse television as well. As a well known musicologist of Sitar & Rudra Veena, he has trained, number of students among whom four worthy students in Veena and Sitar are Prof. Ramchandra V. Hegde, Smt. Jyoti G. Hegde, Prof. Srikant & Dr. Muralidhar Rao (Sitar).

Besides being a musicologist, Dr. Bindu Madhav has also achieved quite a lot in other spheres of life. His other achievements are as follows:-

(i) Educational Qualifications.

M.A — Music

M.A — English.

M.A — Hindi.

C.C — French

PhD. in Music.

(ii) Awards

(a) He is an awardee of the Karnataka State Nrutya Academy, Bangalore, with a title "Karnataka Kala Tilak".

(b) He is also a recipient of the Sri Kanak Purandhar Prashasti, a top most and prestigious award given by the government of Karnataka.

(c) He has also the "Arya Bhat Award, with the title "Sangeet Vidya Prapurna."

(3) Publications

(a) Book:- "Bharatiya Sangeetada Charitre" (Kannada) published by karnataka university, Dharwad.

(b) Book:- Dr. Puttaraj Gawai, published by sangeet Natya Academy, Bangalore.

(4) Research Articles & papers

He has published several articles and research papers in Music, in English, Hindi and Kannada Magazines.

(5) Positions Held

• Head of the Dept. of Music, in M.M. Arts and Science college, Sirsi (U.K) 1963-1980.

• Musicologist and Research Guide in Music and Chairman of post Graduate school of Music in Karnataka University, at Dharwad from 1981 to 1995.

• Member

: Karnataka State Sangeet Nrutya

: Music syllabus Committee, Kala Academy, Panjim, Goa & Karnataka university.

: Board of Studies in Music, Karnataka university, Dharwad.

: Academic Council, Karnataka University, Dharwad.

: Indian Music Congress (W.B)

: Indian Musicological society, Baroda.

: Director, Regional Centre of Research and Development, Karnataka state Sangeet Nratya Academy, Hubli Dharwad

(6)   Guide

(i)   Guide in Music, Dept. of Culture, Ministry of Education and culture, Govt. of India, New Delhi.

(ii) Guide for Ph.D in the Dept, of Music, Karnataka university, Dharwad.

Thus, far five students have got Ph.D award, under his guidance.

Besides the above mentioned Rudra Veena players, there could have been several, whom we may have missed out, we urge other researchers to take up this challenge.

4.5 Styles of Playing Rudra-Veena

The difference of playing Rudra Veena from sitar in that, Rudra Veena is played with two plectrums (mizrabs) while, sitar is played only with one plectrum (mizrab). The Rudra Veena playing styles may be categorized into two categories namely:-

(i)   Dhrupad Baj style and,

(ii) Khyalia Baj style

Let us briefly look into there styles

(i) Dhrupad Baj style
The dhrupad baj style of playing Rudra-Veena was invented by Ustad Vazir Khan & hence it is known by the style the Beenkars play Dhrupad & Dhamar. They are pakhawaj to accompany the Rudra Veena. Some of the great player of Dhrupad baj were Mohammad Ali Khan, Sadat Ali Khan, Kale Khan, Mushruf Khan, Imdad Khan, Lateef Khan, and Waheed Khan.

(ii) The Khyalia baj or Khayal style
The credit for Khyalia style goes to Ustad Bande Ali Khan. Bande Ali Khan the maestro of Been who also knew how to play the Dhrupad style, taught his students the Khyaliia style.

4.6 Current Status of Rudra Veena

Although, over a period of several years, Kings, rishis, munis, and the Rudra Veena players themselves did make efforts to teach their students, it is disheartening to note that as on today there are only two Rudra Veena Maestros namely Dr. Bindu Pathak & pandit Hindraj Divekar. Both pandit Hindraj Divekar and Dr. Bindu Pathak know in & out of the Rudra Veena. Out of the two Dr. Bindu Pathak is almost 65 to 70 years old, thus the only one Maestro of Been left today is Pt. Hindraj Divekar.

Both of them have taught several students, but they are still in the process of learning. They are yet to master the art of playing Rudra Veena from both styles point of view. Ustad

Ziyamoiuddin Dagar who was a Been Maestro, also died recently.

Thus, although the glorious history of Rudra Veena playing originates from India, there are hardly any Maestros of this instrument. When asked some of the players over a period of 15 years of data collectors it was revealed that the traditions of playing Rudra Veena was declining ever the years because of following reasons:-

(i)   The instrument is difficult to play.

(ii)   It is so delicate, that it is difficult to pack it & transport it for concerts.

(iii) Its strings are hard, therefore a player finds it difficult.

(iv)   Its sound, if played without a microphone is very low as compared to a sitar.

(v)   There are hardly any students, who come forward to learn it. People fall for learning sitar, than Rudra Veena.

(vi)   The younger generations is attracted to pop music these days.

(vii) There are hardly any concerts of Rudra Veena in major cities of India.

(viii) The efforts to popularize the instrument is not much. What ever has been made thus for is by the artists only.

(ix)   There are hardly many repairers and makers of Rudra Veena, if one has to buy or repair an already purchased one.

(x)   There is hardly any publicity of the instrument, through literature, media and concerts as well.

Well, that is the Scenario of Rudra Veena currently. This means, a lot needs to be done to preserve Rudra Veena, more than only presenting it once in a while through concerts. We have suggested several strategies to preserve, promote and propagate this little known instrument to the world.

❏ ❏ ❏

5

The Manufacturers of Rudra Veena

The data collected from the Rudra-Veena players by the authors over several years revealed, that some of the important places where Rudra-Veena was manufactured were:-

(i)   Rampur in Uttarpradesh

(ii) Gwalior, Indore, Devas, Bhopal, Barhanpur, Mandav in Madhyapradesh.

(iii) Agra in Delhi.

(iv) Miraj, Ichalkaranji, Kolhapur and pune'in Maharashtra.

(v)   Calcutta from West Bengal.

(vi) Dharwad, Mysore & Hubli in Karnataka.

It is evident from the above places mentioned, that the Rudra Veena was made or manufactured in places, which were centres of kingdoms. This meant that, the role of kings and emperors of the above mentioned places, in promoting the manufacturing of Rudra-Veena, through their makers was pivotal. The royal families, did not only encouraged the musicologists, but also its manufacturers.

But, as time passed by, these small kingdoms declined, with the entry of Britishers in India and later with the formation of independent central and state governments. The establishments of governments gave a new direction to art, music & dance forms. Recognised artists were sent abroad to promote and propagate Indian art. In this process, however the Rudra-Veena, some how did not become popular. This did have an effect on the makers of Rudra Veena.

In this chapter we have presented a case study of the Mirajkar family, originally from Miraj - a place in South Maharashtra, but now settled in Pune. We interviewed Yusuf Mirajkar the owner of Mirajkar shop in Ganpati chowk of Pune city, to trace back the history of Rudra Veena manufacturing. His case study is given below:

5.2   CASE STUDY

Aim of the Case Study
The highlight the status of Rudra Veena manufacturing In India.

Background:

Yusuf Ismail Mirajkar, aged 52, owner of the Mirajkar music instrument shop in Pune, a traditional music instrumental maker from Miraj, located in Southern part of Maharashtra, narrates the status of Rudra Veena makers and manufacturers in India.

Course of Events

Yusuf Ismail Mirajkar, is a member of eighth generation from his family, which has dedicated itself for several decades in making Indian classical musical instruments such as Tambora, Sitar, Veena, Surbahar, Dilruba, Israj, Rudra Veena, Tabla, Harmonium, Dholak etc. The first generation instrument maker from Yusuf's family was late Farid Saheb Satarwala, who lived in Miraj a centre for production of musical instruments.

On enquiring how a Rudra Veena is made, Yusuf said, "It is made from big pumpkins

These pumkins are grown in large quantities in a pilgrimage centre called Pandharpur, located at the Southern part of Maharashtra. The crop is usually harvest in the month of April-May. These pumpkins are dried & cleaned from inside. After this, red cadre wood is fixed on the either ends of two pumpkins, on top of which a hollow bamboo is attached. This bamboo serves as a based for fixing wooden or wax frets. Then, four string are fixed, three of which are brass while one is steel string. After this, side strings are also fixed. Then the dried pumpkins are polished using french polish.

The pumpkins are left for drying for a week or two and then it is ready for sale.

On enquiring why Rudra Veena is not a popular stringed musical instrument, Yusuf said:-

(1) It is not popular, because there is no publicity of the instrument.

(2) Not many concerts are organized in the country these days.

(3) There are less performers of Rudra Veena in the world.

(4) The instrument is difficult to play.

(5) Its strings are thick and hard, hence the performer has to press them hard while playing.

(6) The performer has to place instrument on the shoulder for nearly one to two hours while, performing in a concert. Hence he has to sit in the same posture till he completes a ragh.

(7) People prefer to listen to Sitar than Rudra Veena.

Yusuf has made only 15 Rudra Veenas since last 10 years, and all the 15 have been bought by Westerners, mostly students of pandit Hindraj Divekar. He says Westerners value our musical traditions more than we do.

According to Yusuf, if Rudra Veena has to be preserved, promoted & popularized, the following efforts need to be made.

(1) Encourage the present (living) Maestros by giving them financial support to hold concerts, exhibitions & workshop not only in India, but abroad as well.

(2) Promote Rudra Veena through media.

(3) Preserve it by documeting its glorious part. He added that Pandit Hindraj Divekar and Dr. Robin. D. Tribluwan have made it possible to take Rudra Veena to people through this book.

(4) Since, there are only few performers of Rudra Veena hence, there are less makers or manufacturers of the same. These manufacturers should be also encouraged to train other music instrument makers. Because currently the status of Rudra Veena makers is very disheartening. Yusuf said out of every 350 music instrument makers only, one or two can make Rudra Veena, in India.

Well, that was the case study of Yusuf Ismail Miraj kar from Pune, who have consistently contributed to the making of Rudra Veena for eight generations i.e. almost for three to four hundred years.

ANALYSIS

From the above case study, it is clear that there are hardly few makers and manufacturers of Rudra Veena, who need to be encouraged to train other artists so as to preserve this dealing instrument. More importantly, the performers also need to supported to promote & propagate the instrument & save it from dying a natural death.

As authors of the book, we feel that, there is a need for musicologists to conduct a survey of all the music instrument makers to asses, who amongst them know how to make declining instruments like Rudra Veena. Some of the places & shops known for making Indian classical Musical Instrument are:

(1) Miraj, in Southern Maharashtra

(a) Umar Saheb Satar makers.

(b) Farid Saheb Satar makers.

(c) Mehboob Altaf Satar makers.

(d) Vilayat Husain & brothers.

(e) Bala Saheb Mirajkar.

(f) Abasaheb Satar makers.

(g) Hind Musical Mart.

(h) Anmol Music House.

(i) Bhartiya Tantu Vadya Kendra.

(2) Pune, in Western Maharashtra

(a) Yusuf Ismail Mirajkar, in Ganpati chowk.

(b) Mahendale Music Mart.

(c) Jaswir's shop in Arora towers.

(d) Ismail Mirajkar near Datta temple.

(e) Ajit Musicals Mirajkar, Budhwar peth, near prabhat cinema.

(f)   Navadikar musicals at Tilak Road.

(g)   Modern Music Mart, East street.

(3) Bombay, in Western Maharashtra

(a)   Indian music instrument research centre, Bhulabhai Desai Road, Bombay.

(b)   Raghunath S. Mayekar Sardar V. Patel Road, Bombay.

(c)   Trimurti Musicals, Sainath Market, Malad.

(d)   Om Musicals, Dadar.

(e)   Kartar Music House, Sardar V. Patel Road, Bombay.

Besides the above manufacturers there are several in India. Some of the cities wherein Indian classical Musical Instruments are made, are Calcutta, Indore, Bhopal, Madras, Bhubaneshwar, Patna, Lucknow, Delhi, Gandhinagar, Ahmedabad, Jaipur, Jodhpur, Udaipur etc.

5.3 Well wishers of Rudra Veena

Besides the contributions of Rudra Veena performers & its makers, its well wishers have certainly contributed to its preservation & promotion. In this part of the chapter, we would like to make a mention of late Dr. Harihar Gangadhar Moghe, a medical doctor by profession, but a well wisher of Indian classical Music, himself made a Rudra Veena (Been) in the year 1944. This Been was played with great enthusiasm by the teacher (Guru) of Dr. Moghe late Eknathji Vishnupanth pandit. Eknathji Pandit was a well known singer & a Been player from Gwalior. Pandit Eknathji was a disciple of a well known Been player from Delhi namely "Niyamat Khan". Dr. Moghe, thus, not only had a reputation of a recognised medical doctor in Bombay, but he was good musician too. More importantly, he was the only disciple of pandit Eknathji. Dr. Moghe did play Been. The above information has been reported by Dr. Shashikala N. Gore, from 12 Vishnu Sadan, 1148, Sadashiv Peth Pune, in her article captioned, "Ade Madadev Been Bajaye, which appeared in Maharashtra Times (Marathi paper), dated 22nd, June 1986. The photo graph of Been personally made by Dr. Moghe is in the picture section of the book.

Yet another well wisher & a performer of Been, S.W. Jitendra from London, who is a disciple of Pandit Hindraj Divekar made a Been in the year 1974. S. W. Jitendra infact made, two Beens., all by himself, under the guidance of Pt. Divekar. He would play these instruments in Himalaya and in the caves of Ellora in India.

Late Dr. Moghe from Bombay & S.W. Jeetendra from London are two examples of people who made efforts to make Rudra Veena. We as authors feel that there may be several such wishers about when there is no information. Nevertheless, it is necessary to document the efforts of such people, who definitely contributed in saving the declining tradition of Rudra Veena.

6

Efforts To Preserve and Popularize Rudra Veena

6.1 Role of Rishis (Hermits) and Munis

The credit for manufacturing playing & preserving Veena during the vedic period centuries ago, goes to the rishis & munis, who uses the instrument for devotion. This instrument, then must have been a considered to be a sacred one, as it was an invention of Lord Shiva. The Rudra Veena was perhaps popular in the temples then. We therefore feel that the rishis & munis played a vital role in preserving this ancient instrument.

There is a myth about how the rishis (Hermits) use to play Rudra-Veena for meditation. Several centuries ago, a hermit used to teach 200 students the art of Rudra-Veena in a cave in Himalayan Mountain ranges in North India. The instrument was used for devotion & meditation.

Once, while he was teaching his students, he was playing the Rudra-Veena, so melodiously, that every one was engrossed in hearing the same. So much so, that because of the sweetness of the melody of Rudra-Veena, the cave was automatically closed & the hermit with his two hundred students took samadhi. That is, they died while, playing devotional music.

Some of the names worth mentioning are Bharata, Adi, Kohala Bharata, Matanga Bharata, during the Vedic period contributed in preserving the art of Rudra-Veena. It was at this time when Bharata Muni classified the seven notes Sa, Re, Ga, Ma, Pa, Dha, Ni, into Shadja, Rishaba, Gandhara, Madhyama, Panchama, Dhaivata & Nishada. Yet another person's name is worth mentioning & that is Bharata sen Dattila, who wrote a book called "Dattilam". This piece of work was a scientific effort to put on record the essence of Indian classical Music during Vedic period. Similarly, another writer by the name Matanga, flourished during this time. He wrote a book called "Brihdeshi, around 8th century in which we find a mention of Raghas.

Yet another thing happened during the vedic period and that was the formation of caste system, which is based on the four varnas namely Brahmana, Kshatriya, Vaishya & Shudra. Caste groups then, were classified on an hierarchical base & assigned people with certain occupation & social duties & responsibilities for the functioning of Hindu society. The art of learning music too was assigned to certain castes. In Maharashtra the Brahmans (Priest) and Gurav castes (temple case takers) are known for playing devotional music. In other states of India too, there are caste groups who play devotional & aesthetic music. Thus, a particular caste to which a social responsibility of playing an instrument(s) was assigned they, may have continued the tradition as time passed by. The pakhawaj (drum) - an ancient rhythm instrument, is still played in the rural & even urban temples of Maharashtra by the Gurav Community artists.

Since, the social responsibility such as playing devotional music by a caste group was believed to be a divine sanction, it was perhaps treasured, over the years.

6.2 Role of Kings, Emperors & Princes

If one analyses the continuity of Indian classical music over the years, he comes to a conclusion, that after the rishis & munis, the royal personalities, were responsible for preserving, inventing & promoting music. We believe that the entry of Moghuls in India was a boon to Indian classical music, because a lot of new variety of musical styles & the instruments were invented then.

Not to forget the contribution of Amir Khusro - a statesman and a musician in the courts of Khiljis & Tughlaks, who invented the Sitar & tabla. These instruments are really appreciated throughout the world today. Later on some of the famous personalities in music were Miya Tensen, Baiju Bawara, Nayak Gopal, Ramdas, during the reign of Akbar, deserve a word of praise.

In fact Emperor Akbar had employed as many as thirty six experts in his court, in the field of art & music. Thus, the role of Maghul kings, emperors & princess is of great significance when it comes to preservation & promotion of Rudra-Veena along with other instruments as well.

Even after the Britishers took over India, small Kingdoms, which still had royal families, did encourage musicians & the manufacturers of musical instruments. Some of the names of Kingdoms are worth mentioning. These are Mysore from South, Miraj, Pune & Kolhapur from Maharashtra, Devas, Allahabad; Delhi & Agra from Uttarpradesh; Indore, Gwalior, Mandav, Ujjain, Jhansi, Bhopal etc. from Madhyapradesh, Jaipur, Udaipur, Jodhpur, Chittor, etc. from Rajasthan, Baroda & Ahmedabad from Gujarat, Calcutta from West Bengal, Bhubaneshwar from Orissa & so on. These kingdoms and the Royal personalities associated with it, were fond of music & promoted it to the best of their abilities.

Rudra-Veena is no exception to the rule. If the readers of this book read biographies of famous Rudra-Veena players given in chapter four, they will get an impression that most Beenkars played in the courts of the Indian kings. For example Late Ustad Bande Ali Khan played in the court of Indore Kings, Late Ustad Rajab Ali Khan played in the court of Kolhapur Maharaj in South Maharashtra from 1895 to 1915, for almost 20 years; Late Pandit Krishna Rao Kolhapure played in the Baroda sansthan; Late Pandit Hindagandharva Shivram Divekar used to play in the court of Mysore, whenever called by the Maharaja. This proves, that the Royal families of small kingdoms did play a vital role in preservation, promotion & propagation of Rudra-Veena.

6.3 Role of Rudra-Veena Artists

Despite of the moral, financial & religious support from the Indian society, finally it was the player or performer, who is considered to be the soul of continuity of Rudra Veena tradition. They served as oxygen cylinders to pump into life the declining instrument & the tradition as it were.

Thus, right from vedic times the Rishis & Munis like Bharata, Nandikeshwara, Markendya, Purana, Vayu Purana, Matanga, Narada, Isana Bana Bharata did contribute to playing, preservation & promotion of Rudra Veena. During the Moghul rule, names like Tansen Miya, Baiju Bawara, Nayak Gopal, Amir Khusro who played Rudra Veena and contributed to its preservation & promotion need a word of praise.

Of course from 1840 onwards great maestros like Late Ustad Bande Ali Khan; Late Ustad Wazir Khan, Late Ustad Murad Khan; Late Ustad Krishnarao Majumdar, Late Chunnabai; Late Ustad Rajab Ali Khan, Late Ustad Babu Khan, Late Pandit Krishna rao Kolhapure, Late pandit Krishna Rao Palande, Late pandit Dattopant pathak, Late Ustad Abdul Karim Khan, Late pandit Acharekar, Late Ustad Ziyamoiuddin Dagar, Late Pandit Hindagandharva Shivrambuva Divekar and of course the living maestros Pt. Pandharinath Kolhapur, Pt. Hindraj Divekar, Dr. Bindu Madhav Pathak dedicated their lives to the cause of Rudra-Veena.

6.4   Role of Drama Companies and Actors

While collecting data on the historical aspects of Rudra Veena, it was observed that, besides Rishis, munis, kings the performers of Rudra Veena themselves, drama company owners & actors did contribute to a great extent in promotion & propagation of Rudra-Veena.

For example the Balwant Sangeet Mandali, a drama Company owned by Late Master Dinanath Mangeshkar the father of Lata Mangeshkar; Late Pandit Krishna Rao Kolhapure the grandfather of famous actress Padmini Kolhapure, requested Late Ustad Murad Khan to teach Late Krishna Rao Kolhapure the art playing Rudra-Veena. Infact the credit to do so goes to Late Master Dinanath Mangeshkar, the main trustee of Balwant Sangeet Mandali. He asked Pandit Krishnarao Kolhapur to learn Rudra Veena & he was responsible to Summon Ustad Murad Khan to be part of the drama company.

If it were not for Master Dinanath Mangeshkar's efforts there would not have been a single Beenkar from Bande Ali Khan's tradition in Maharashtra. Because Pandit Krishan Rao Kolhapure, Pandit Krishna Rao Palande from Dharwad & Pandit Datto pant, pathak could take advantage of Ustad Murad's presence. We the authors of this book pay our respect to this famous actor of Marathi stage actor & singer, Late, Master Dinanath Mangeshkar, born on 29th December, 1899 and died on 24th April, 1942, for his contribution to upliftment of Rudra Veena. By the way the Balwant Sangeet Mandal was established in the year January, 1918 and closed down on 15th June, 1933.

6.5 Late Natasrestha Chintoba Gurav (Divekar's) Contribution

Before getting into the contribution of Late Natasrestha Chintoba Gurav (Divekar's) contribution in preservation, promotion & propatation of Rudra Veena, let us first understand who he was. Chintoba Gurav was born on December 22, 1874 & started his career as an actor since he was ten years old. He was the first, person in India to start a drama company in the year 1913. As a Director of drama, popularity called "Taleem Master", those days, chintoba worked for the Kiroloskar Natak company as a Director, the Balwant Sangeet Mandali, Rajaram Sangeet Mandali, Yashwant Sangeet Mandali, Balgandharva Sangeet Mandali and so on.

Among the prominent disciples or students of Late Natasrestha chintoba Divekar are well known actor & singer Lata Mangeshkar Late Master Dinanath Mangeshkar, Late Hirabai

Barodekar, Late Balgandharva, Late Mugubai Kurdikar, Late Yallubai Mane, Late Natvarya Bapurao Mane, Vasant Shinde, Sharad Talwalkar and others.

During those days he was a famous singer and an actor-cum Director. Some of his famous dramas are, Sangeet Sharda, Soubhadra, Shapsam Bhram, Manapman, Punya Prabhav, Sanshayakallol, Dambhasphot etc.

It was in the year 1942 that chintoba was honoured before a huge audience gathered for drama festival at charni road, in Bombay. Chintoba was awarded a sum of Rs. 1,500/- by Late Balgandharva collected by both Acharya Atre & Bal gandharva himself from the audience.

In the similar festival organized in Delhi in 1955, he was honoured by late prime Minister of India, Pandit Jawahar Lal Nehru. Thus, as an actor, Director & a great singer of his time Late Natasrestha Chintoba Gurav (Divekar) was very famous personality in the country.

As regards his role in preserving, promoting and propagating Rudra Veena, he did his level best to promote Rudra Veena. He started the same with his own home. He instructed his own Son Shivrambuva Divekar to learn from Pandit Krishna Rao Kolhapure & Pandit Acharekar. Because he instructed his Son Shivram buva, Chintoba's grandson Pt. Hindraj Divekar was initiated in Rudra-Veena. Because Pt. Hindraj was trained to play Rudra Veena for over 27 years, he could propagate it abroad.

Besides instructing his son & grandson to take up playing of Rudra Veena, Chintoba also created a platform for propagating the same in the courts of various kings in India, those days. He would take either pandit Krishnarao Kolhapure or his own son Pandit Hindgandharva Shivrambuva Divekar to play Rudra Veena in the courts of Indian Maharaja's, whenever he was called by them to sing or act in their courts. Thus, this great "son of Marathi stage", gave one hundred percent not only to drama, singing, acting but to the continuity of Rudra Veena tradition as well.

6.6 Efforts of Prof. B.R. Deodhar

The credit to broadcast Rudra Veena on All India Radio for the first time in the History of the instrument goes to Prof. B.R. Deodhar from Bombay. In the year 1927 Ustad Murad Khan's programmes & Rudra Veena concerts were organized by Prof. Deodhar. He also for the first time took Ustad Murad Khan to the All India Radio Station & broadcasted his Been on air. Prof. Deodhar had a music academy, wherein Ustad Murad Khan was requested to teach Rudra Veena, in Bombay. Thus, Prof. B.R. Deodhar's name will always remain on records for his efforts to popularize Rudra Veena.

6.7 Popularizing Rudra Veena Abroad

Among the many maestros of Rudra Veena, the credit to popularize Rudra Veena abroad goes first to Pandit Hindraj Divekar & Late Ustad Ziyamoiuddin Dagar. It was in the year 1979 that Pandit Hindraj Divekar rendered his first concert abroad in Perth, Adeliade, Melbourne & Sydney in Australia. He also performed in Germany, Italy & France. Late Ustad Ziyamoiuddin rendered Rudra-Veena concerts in Europe & America.

6.8 Well Wishers & Performers of Rudra Veena Abroad.

As mentioned above the credit to popularize Rudra Veena goes to Pt. Divekar & Late Ustad Ziyamoiuddin Dagar. Their efforts were supported by their Been & Sitar students from abroad.

For Pandit Hindraj Divekar, his students Sayer and Jaison who organized concerts in Australia; Dr. Horst Rolly organized concerts in Germany and Dr. Iris Schneller and Swami sangeet organized concerts in Italy & France. The concerts in of Late Ziyamoiuddin Dagar were organized in Europe & America by his students Philip Brugier, Lokombe and Dr. Kim Wardroof. Besides organizing concerts the students of Pt. Hindraj Divekar are also teaching interested youngsters Rudra Veena abroad. He has his students in Germany, America, Canada, Taiwan, Isreal, Australia, Germany, Spain, Malaysia, Japan, England, Switzerland, Newzeland and India as well. It is surprising to note that the westerners are taking keen interest in learning Indian Music & propagating it abroad, for the last 3 to 4 decades.

6.9 Propagation through Audio Tapes

The credit for audio recording of Rudra Veena goes to Prof. B.R. Deodhar in 1928, H.M.V a music company, Late Ustad Ziyamoiuddin Dagar, Dr. Horst Rolly from Germany in 1983, Philip Brugier from France, and finally to Dr. Robin D Tribhuwan, an Anthropologist, produced in audio tape captioned, "Rudra Veena" — An Ancient Instrument, in the year 1999. The artist who has played for the tape is none other but Pt. Hindraj Divekar. Efforts of these people in preserving, popularizing & upgrading the Rudra Veena will always be placed on record, in the history of Indian classical music.

6.10 A word of Respect to the Manufacturers

Last, but not the least, we would like to place on record the tidious efforts of all the Rudra Veena manufacturers right from the vedic terms until now. For, if it were not their interest & efforts to make the instrument it would have been difficult for the performers to play it.

6.11 This Book on Rudra Veena: A Land Mark

This written & published document, which is a tidious sincere & honest effort of the authors for several years will remain as a treasure in literature. Secondly it would serve as a methodological & theoretical guide for researchers in music and Ethnco-musicicology to take up research on the unknown and little known traditions of music in India. We hope that, it would be a starting land mark to evoke interest among young scholars.

6.12 Role of Doordharshan and All India Radio

The Doordhan T.V. channel has telecasted Rudra Veena live, played by Divekar. The Kamataku Doordarshan has also telecasted performance of Late Datto Pant Pathak's recently his living son's performance as well, Dr. Bindu Pathak. The credit for broad carting Rudra Veena goes to All India Radio too.

6.13 Role of Surabhi cultural & Research Foundation

The Surabhi cultural & Research Foundation, headed by Sidharth Kak, has documented visual & live performance of Rudra Veena, so as to popularize & preserve the same.

❏ ❏ ❏

Makers of Rudra Veena

While, on one hand the Rudra Veena players contributed in preserving the instrument, on the other hand, its makers put life in it. Given here are photo graphs of Farid Saheb, Husen Saheb and Umar Saheb of the Mirajkar family who made Rudra Veena and supplied them to Musicians and Royal Courts in 18th and early 19th century.

Farid Saheb Mirajkar who lived during Bande Ali Khan's times, in the early 18th century. He established the Mirajkar Musical instrument manufacturing unit at Miraj.

Husen Saheb Miraj Kar who
lived in late 18th century was a
instrument maker of Mirajkar
family.

Umar Saheb Mirajkar

Rudra Veena of Late Ustad Bande Ali Khan (Courtsy Raja Kelkar Musium, Pune)

Rudra Veena of Late Ustad Bande Ali Khan (Courtsy Raja Kelkar Musium, Pune)

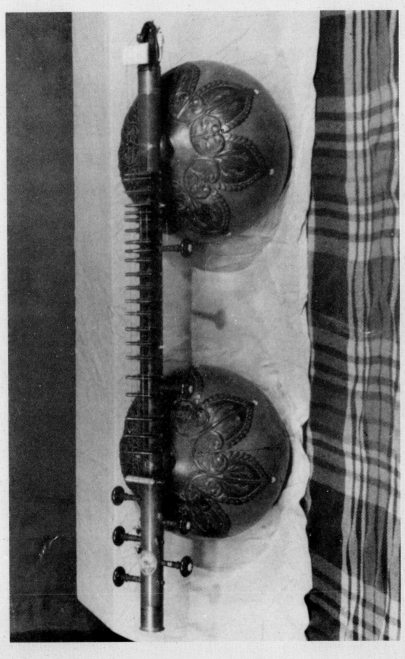

Rudra Veena Made personally by late Dr. Harihar Gangadhar Moghe in the year 1944. He made another one in 1950. (Courtsy Dr. Shashikala Gore-the grand-daughter of Dr. Moghe).

Pandit Hindraj Divekar in the Centre playing the hundred years old Rudra Veena bought by his father late Hindagandharva Pandit Shivrambuva Divekar from a Muslim Beenkar.

Mr. Yusuf Ismail Miraj Kar, from Pune, who originally is a native of Miraj has been making Rudra Veena for several years. He is a member of eighth generation of Rudra Veena makers in his family.

Yusuf Mirajkar seen Repairing Pandit Hindraj Divekar's Rudra Veena.

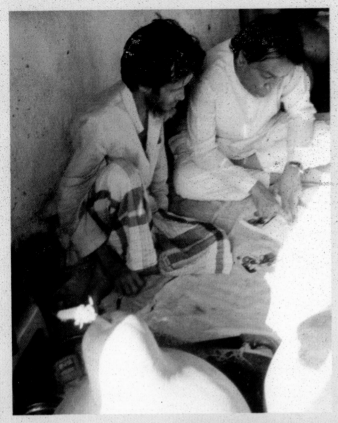

Late Mehaboob
one of the
expert Rudra
Veena makers
who worked for
Farid Saheb
Sitar makers in
Miraj.

Pandit Hindraj Divekar
giving instructions to
Mehboob before making a
new Rudra Veena.

Rudra Veena's made by Mehaboob.

S.W. Jitendra from London, a student of Pandit Hindraj made this Rudra Veena in the year 1974.

S.W. Jitendra made yet another Rudra Veena in 1975.

S.W. Jitendra playing the Rudra Veena in a village near Himalaya.

S.W. Jitendra playing the Rudra Veena at Ellora.

Late Ustad Bande Ali Khan a Maestro of Rudra Veena.

Late Chunnabai–the student of Bande Ali Khan is the only known Rudra Veena played and a court singer in the 18th century.

Late Ustad Murad Khan Rudra Veena
player and a student of Bande Ali Khan.

Late Pandit Krishnarao Kolhapure
Rudra Veena (Been) player–a student
of Ustad Murad Khan.

Late Pandit Gangadhar Achrekar Rudra
Veena plaer and a writter.

Late Hindgandharva Pandit
Shivrambuva Divekar–a well known
Rudra Veena player, an acter and a
vocalist.

Late Hindgandharva Pandit Shivram buva Divekar being felicitated by the then honourable prime Minister of India Shri Morarji Desai (13-3-1987) in Pune.

Late Pandit Dattapant pathak a well known Rudra Veena player from Hubli-Karnataka.

Pandit Hindraj Divekar playing Rudra Veena.

Pandit Pandharinath
Kolhapure–Rudra
Veena player and a
singer from Bombay.

Dr. Bindumadhav Pathak a Rudra
Veena player from Hubli.

Dr. Ian Duncan from Italy learning Rudra Veena from Pt. Hindraj Divekar.

Mrs. Joshi of Doordarshan taking Pt. Hindraj's interview for the Television.

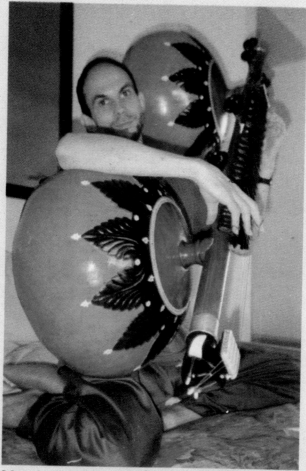

Mr. Mitto from Switzerland–a student of Pandit Hindraj Divekar.

A clock presented to Chintoba Divekar by
the then Maharaja of Kolhapur Shahu Maharaj.

Pandit Hindraj performing in Heidelberg–Germany.

Pandit Hindraj is accompanied by Pandit Sadananda on tabla and Raju Shahane with tanpura at a music festival in Bombay.

Pandit Hindraj is a Maestro of Sitar as well. He is accompanied by Padmakar Gujar with Tabla and Mrs. Gauri Divekar with Tanpura.

The Tomb of Late great Ustad Bande Ali Khan in front of Shaniwar Wada on the bank of the River.

Late Bande Ali Khan's Tomb showing his death 27-7-1895.

Late Nata Srestha Chintoba Divekar (Gurur)–a force of inspiration to the Divekars for taking up Rudra Veena.

A Woman playing Rudra Veena on an elephant—A painting during Moghul rule.

7

Summary And Conclusions

(7.1) **Rudra Veena** — An Ancient Instrument, the continuity of which went through ups and downs in the history of Indian classical Instruments, is a rare instrument. Today its current status reveals that there are hardly any maestros of the same. Infact Pt. Hindraj Divekar is the only living artist of the two surviving, who is rendering Rudra-Veena concerts, not only in India, but abroad as well.

In order to popularize this instrument with reference to its status, continuity and charge right from vedic times to date this book has been written. The authors documented valuable data on musical, Anthropological sociological, and historical aspects of the instrument and its traditions for several years.

The main aim to publish this book is to, remind the young scholars to take up studies on such unknown instruments and their traditions. Secondly the book also provides methodological and theoretical insights, on the lines of which research studies can be taken up.

The book is presented in seven chapters as follows:-

(i) An overview of music and musical traditions in India;

(ii) Research Methodology;

(iii) Types of Indian classical Musical Instruments;

(iv) Place of Rudra Veena in Indian classical music;

(v) The Manufacturers of Rudra Veena;

(vi) Efforts to Popularize Rudra Veena;

(vii) Summary & conclusions.

From the analysis of the qualitaive data gathered certain impressions and conclusions were drawn. These are as follows:

(7.2) Conclusions

(1) During pre-vedic and vedic times Rudra Veena survived in the temples and at the hands of Rishis and Munis, because of the divine and mythological significance attached to it.

(2)   The Moghul emperors and Sultans especially Allauddin Khilji, the Tughlaks and Emperor Akbar revitalized the playing and manufacturing of Rudra Veean by encouraging performers & its makers.

(3)   Although the instrument mythologically is a creation of Hindus, it was nurtured by the Muslim rulers and players, from 13th century to end of 19th century.

(4)   Rudra Veena did suffer a set back during the British rule.

(5)   Besides Rishis, Munis and Kings the credit for preserving Rudra Veena goes to Drama companies, its makers, people who recorded and popularized it & actors who propagated it.

(6)   The instrument did not become popular in the 20th century for following reasons:-

(i)   The instrument is difficult to play.

(ii)   It is so delicate that it is hard to transport it for concerts.

(iii) Its strings are harder as compared to sitar.

(iv) Its sound, if played without a microphone is very low as compared to sitar.

(v)   There are hardly any students, who come forward to learn it. People fall for learning sitar, than Rudra-Veena.

(vi) The younger generation is attracted to pop music these days. Where as to hear or play Rudra Veena, one has to have patience, which today's youngsters lack.

(vii) There are hardly any concerts of Rudra-Veena in major cities of India, and abroad as well.

(viii)A lot of people have still not heard about Rudra-Veena is.

(xi) people who want to posses one, fear to buy it because there are hardly many repairers & makers of Rudra-Veena. Secondly, there are only few places, where the instrument is manufactured and repaired. Therefore to avoid travelling long distance for such a delicate instrument people do not fall for it.

(x)   Older the Rudra Veena, the better Museum piece it becomes. Instead of continuing playing on it, relatives & well wishers of deceased Rudra Veena players prefer to hand over the piece to the Museum.

(xi) There is very less, infact no publicity of Rudra Veena among the younger generations.

(xii) The performer has to sit straight for hours with the Rudra Veena on his shoulders while performing. To a beginner it is a painful task.

(xiii)The process of making a Rudra Veena is long and tidious.

(7)   The Westerners are getting attracted to Indian music these days and hence in whatever small way Rudra Veena is paving its way to popularity in the west.

(8)   Over the years Rudra Veena artists have made changes in the structure & audio presentability of the instrument. For example the idea of putting in a small microphone into the gourd was an invention of Late Pt. Hindagandharva Shivram Divekar and his son Pt. Hindraj Divekar. The size of the frets was changed by Late Ustad Ziyamoiuddin

Dogar. He also increased the number of strings.

(9) String instruments such as sitar, Mendolin, Santoor, Sarangi & Swar mandal which are more melodious than the Rudra-Veena are in great demand from the audience.

(10) The artists of Rudra-Veena therefore had to face a defeat as compared to other string instrument performers in the world of music and market competition.

7.3) Recommendations

Given this background, we, Pt. Hindraj Divekar and Dr. Robin D. Tribhuwan as authors of this book would like to make following recommendations to music academies, government and cultural developmental Departments and, concerned international organizations, museums & well wishers of music, that:

(i) Efforts should be made to encourage more inter-disciplinary research studies on the unknown & little known music instruments & traditions, by offering fellowships and scholarships to musicologists & researchers.

(ii) Instruments which are declining or have become rare, should be recorded & video taped to preserved their sound.

(iii) Living artists of unknown or little known musical instruments & traditions should be encouraged for concerts, workshops, exhibitions & demonstrations both in India & abroad.

(iv) The school & college going youngsters should be exposed to such musical traditions through exhibitions and lectures.

(v) Financial assistance should be provided to publish books to researchers working on such rare topics.

(vi) The concerts & demonstrations of such rare musical instruments should be telecasted & broadcasted so as to give it fame.

(vii) Seminars, workshops and conferences should be organized very frequently so as to provide a platform for musicians and scholars to meet, discuss & develop insights into such rare subjects.

(viii) Fusion of Eastern & Western instruments should be promoted so as to popularize Indian Instruments Abroad. For example the fusion of Sitar played by Pt. Hindraj Divekar with clarinet played by Bandoba Solapurkar, sounds so melodious. They have been rendering these kind of concerts, through out Maharashtra.

(ix) Film Institutes, Educational Media Research centres (EMRC) should make efforts to trace unknown & known musical traditions and make films to educate people. Infact film makers should be encouraged by giving them financial incentives to make films on such topics.

(x) Music institutions & organizations should make efforts to organize demonstrations in schools & colleges.

(xi) The Rotary & Lions club can play a vital role in organizing concerts of Rudra Veena artists.

(xii) Exhibitions on such topics should be organized.

REFERENCES

(1) Marsh Robert, 1981. Music, in the World Book Encyclopaedia, (M. Vol. 13), world book child craft International Inc. Chicago.

(2) Engel Hans, 1968, Music & society, in the International Encyclopaedia of social sciences, Vol. X, the Macmillan company & Free press, U.S.A.

(3) Merriam Allan P, 1968 Music: Ethnomusicology, in the International Encyclopaedia of Social Science Vol. X, the Macmillan company & Free press, U.S.A.

(4) Bhattacharya Dilip, 1999 Musical Instruments of Tribal India, Manas publications, New Delhi.

(5) Bala Gopal Tara, 1981. Learn to play on veena, pankaj publications, New Delhi.

(6) Krishna Swami, 1965 Musical Instruments of India, publications Division, Ministry of Information & Broadcasting, New Delhi.

(7) Joshi G.N. 1977. Understanding Indian classical Music, Tarapore vala, Bombay.

(8) Tribhuwan Robin & Tribhuwan preeti 1999 Tribal Dances of India, Discovery publishing House, New Delhi.

(9) Ranade Ashok, 1986, Parmeshwaradin pratik Manali, Geleei, in Sakal Newspaper, May 15, 1986 Thursday, June.

(10) Sawant Sulekha, 1984 An Article in Marathi language, appeared in Maharashtra Times, News paper pune, dated 9th Dec. 1984.

(11) Deodhar B.R. 1953, Murad Khan — Beenkar, in sangeet kala vihar, (Marathi Magazine), July issue Gayanan publishing House, Miraj.

(12) Shashikala Gore,

Ade Mahadev Been Bajai, Marashtra Times News paper, dated 22nd June, 1986, Pune.

❏ ❏ ❏

APPENDIX

TOPIC — RUDRA VEENA — AN ANCIENT STRING MUSICAL INSTRUMENT

RESEARCHERS — PANDIT HINDRAJ DIVEKAR & DR. ROBIN D. TRIBHUWAN

Interview Schedule

No. 1

(For Rudra Veena Players)

Personal Information

1. Name

2. Sex

3. Age

4. Education

5. Religion

6. Caste/Tribe

7. Martial Status

8. Annual Income

9. No. of Family Members

   (a) Males

   (b) Females

   (c) Total

10. Address

11. Since how many years are you playing Rudra Veena?

12. Who initiated you into playing it ?

13. What else do you play ?

14. Which Rudra Veena tradition or Gharana do you belong to ?

15. How many students do you have ?

16. What style do you play, on Rudra veena ?

17. How old is this instrument ?

18. How was it preserved, promoted & propagated ?

19. Where all have you rendered Rudra Veena concerts in India & Abroad ?

20. Was there a female Rudra Veena player in the past ?

21. What are the reasons for unpopularity of Rudra Veena ?

22. What according to you should be done to preserve the same ?

23. Can you tell us something about recording of this instrument ?

24. Do you know any manufacturers & makers of Rudra Veena ?

25. What was your contributions to preservation of Rudra Veena ?

26. Any other Relevant Information.

61

TOPIC — RUDRA VEENA — AN ANCIENT STRING MUSICAL INSTRUMENT

RESEARCHER — PANDIT HINDRAJ DIVEKAR & DR. ROBIN. D. TRIBHUWAN

Interview schedule

No. 2

(For Manufacturers of Rudra Veena)

(I)   Personal Informations

1.   Name

2.   Sex

3.   Age

4.   Education

5.   Religion

6.   Caste/tribe

7.   Annual Income

8.   Marital Status

9.   No. of Family Members

    (a) Males

    (b) Females

    (c) Total

10.   Address

11.   Since how many years are you making musical instruments ?

12.   No. of generations in this business ?

13.   Who in your family first started making musical instruments ?

14.   Which instruments were made then ?

15.   Who in your family first made Rudra Veena ?

16.   When was it ? (Year)

17.   How was it made ?

18.   Who would order Rudra Veenas from you then ?

19.   Who orders Rudra Veenas from you now ?

20.   Is there a special Rudra Veena maker in your shop ?

21.   His detailed Information.

22.   How many Rudra Veenas did you make thus far ?

23.   Where all in India did you sell Rudra Veena ?

24. Could you please give brief information about your Rudra Veena clients ?

25. What is the procedure of making Rudra Veena ?

26. What is the current status of production and sale of Rudra Veena.

27. Which other modern and ancient instruments do you make ?

28. What strategies do you suggest to promote & propagate Rudra Veena in India and Abroad ?   ❑ ❑ ❑

Lessons From Rudra Veena

For the sake of those individuals, interested in learning Rudra Veena we have made a provisions by giving lessons of ten raghas. These ten raghas are: Yaman, Bhup, Brindavani, Bagashri, Bihag, Mal Kaunse, Puriya Kalyan, Darbari Kanda, Miya Malhar and Bhairavi. Detailed lesson of every ragh is given in English as well as in Hindi. We hope that these lessons will be of some help to the beginers of Rudra Veena.

LESSONS FROM RUDRA VEENA

TEN RAGHAS

(1) Yaman

Aroha—	Ni	Re	Ga	Ma	Gha	Ni	Sả	
Avroha—	Sa	Ni	Dha	Pa	Ma	Ga	Re	Sa	

(2) Bhup

Aroha—	Sa	Re	Ga	Pa	Dha	Sả	
Avroha—	Sa	Dha	Pa	Ga	Re	Sa	

(3) Brindavani Sarang

Aroha—	Sa	Re	Ma	Pa	Ni	Sả	
Avroha—	Sả	Ni	Pa	Ma	Re	Sa	

(4) Bageshri

Aroha—	Sa	Ga	Ma	Dha	Ni	Sả		
Avroha—	Sả	Ni	Dha	Ma	Ga	Re	Sa	

(5) Bihag

Aroha—	Ni	Sa	Ga	Ma	Pa	Ni	Sả	
Avroha—	Sa	Ni	Dha	Pa	Ma			
		Pa	Ga	Ma	Ga	Re	Sa	

(6) Malkuanse

Aroha—	Sa	Ga	Ma	Dha	Ni	Sa	
Avroha—	Sa	Ni	Dha	Ma	Ga	Sả	

(7)   **Puriya Kalyan or Purva Kalyan**

Aroha— Sa   Re   Ga   Må   Pa   Dha   Ni   Sa |

Avroha— Sa   Ni   Dha   Pa   Ma   Ga   Sa |

(8)   **Darbari Kanda**

Aroha— Sa   Re   Ga   Ma   Pa   Dha   Ni   Så |

Avroha— Sa   Dha   Ni   Pa   Ma   Pa   Ga   Ma   Re

Sa |

(9)   **Miya Malhar**

Aroha— Sa   Re   Re   Pa   Ma   Ni   Dha   Ni   Så |

Avroha— Så   Dha   Ni   Pa   Ma   Ga   Ma   Re   Sa |

(10)   **Bhairavi**

Aroha— Sa   Re   Ga   Ma   Pa   Dha   Ni   Så |

Avroha— Sa   Ni   Dha   Pa   Ma   Ga   Re   Sa |

1

RAGH-YAMAN

TAL-TRITAL

(1)	1	2	3	4		5	6	7	8		9	10	11	12		13	14	15	16
														Ni		Re	Ga	—	Re

	Ga	—	—	—		Ga	Re	Ga	Må		Ga	Re	Sa	—	
(2)											Ni	Re	Ga	Re	

	Ga	—	Ma	—		Pa	—	Ma	—		Re	—
(3)											Ni	Re	Ga	— Re

Ga	—	—	Ni		Re	Ga	—	Re		Ga	—	—	Ni		Re	Ga	—	Re

Tode or Variation

(1)	—	—	—	—		Må	Dha	Ni	Sa		Ma	Dha	Ni	Sa		Sa	Ni	Dha	Pa
	Ma	Dha	Ni	Sa		Ni	Re	Sa	—		Ni	Re	Sa	Ga		Ma	—	—	—

(2)	—	—	—	—		Ma	Dha	Ni	Sa		Dha	Ni	Sa	Re		Re	Sa	Ni	Dha
	Ma	Dha	Ni	Sa		Ni	Re	Sa	—		Ni	Re	Sa	Ga		Ma	—	—	—

(3)	—	—	—	—		Ni	Re	Ga	Må		Re	Ga	Må	Pa		Pa	Må	Ga	Re
	Må	Ga	Re	Sa		Ni	Re	Sa	—		Dha	Ni	Sa	—		Ga	Ma	

(4)	—	—	—	—		Ni	Re	Ga	Ga		Ni	Re	Ga	Ga		Ma	Ga	Re	Sa
	Må	Ga	Re	Sa		Ma	Dha	Ni	Sa		Ni	Re	Sa	Ga		Ma		

(5)	—	—	—	—		Ni	Re	Ga	Må		Re	Ga	Må	Pa		Ga	Må	Pa	Dha
	Pa	Må	Ga	Re		Ma	Dha	Ni	Sa		Ni	Re	Sa	—		Ga	Ma	—	—

(6)	—	—	—	—		Ni	Re	Ga	Ma		Dha	Ni	Sa	—		Sa	Ni	Dha	Pa
	Må	Ga	Re	Sa		Ni	Re	Sa	—		Ni	Re	Sa	—		Ga	Ma	—	—

2
RAGH - BHUP

TAL—TRITAL

(1) 1   2   3   4 | 5   6   7   8 | 9   10 11 12 | 13 14 15 16
                                | Ga Pa Ga Re | Sa Dha Sa Re |

Ga — — — | Ga Re Sa —

(2) | Dha Dha Sa — | Dha Dha Sa — |

Sa Re Ga Pa | Ga Re Sa — |

(3)   Ga Pa Ga Re | Sa Dha Sa Re |

Ga Pa Ga Re | Sa Dha Sa Re | Ga Pa Ga Re | Sa Dha Sa Re |

Tode or Variation

(1) — — — —| Pa Dha Sa Re | Pa Dha Sa Re | Re Sa Dha Pa |

Pa Dha Sa Re| Dha Re Sa — | Ga Ma — — | — — — — |

(2) — — — —| Pa Dha Sa Re | Dha Sa Re Ga | Ga Re Sa Dha |

Re Sa Dha Pa| Dha Re Sa — | Ga Ma — — — — |

(3) — — — —| Sa Re Ga Ga | Sa Re Ga Ga | Re Ga Pa Pa

Re Ga Pa Pa| Pa Ga Re Sa | Ga Ma — — — — |

(4) — — — —| Sa Re Ga Pa | Re Ga Pa Pa | Pa Ga Re Sa

Pa Dha Sa Re| Ga Re Sa — | Ga Ma — — | — |

(5) — — — —| Sa Re Ga Pa | Dha Dha Sa — | Sa Dha Pa Ga |

Ga Re Sa —| Dha Re Sa — | Ga Ma — — | — — — — |

3
RAGH - SARANG (BRINDAVANI)

TAL-TRITAL

```
      1   2   3   4 | 5   6   7   8 | 9  10  11  12 | 13  14  15  16 |

(1)                                           Ma |  Re  Nị  —   Sa |
      Nị  —   —   — | Pa  —   Ni  — | Re  Sa  —    | Ga  Ma   —   — |
(2)                                        Nị |  Sa  Pa   —  Nị |
      Sa  —   Re  — | Ma  —   Pa  Ma| Re  Sa  —   —   —   —   —    |
(3)                                           Ma |  Re  Nị  —   Sa |
      Nị  —   —  Ma| Re  Ni  —   Sa| Nị  —   —  Ma | Re  Nị   —  Sa |
      Nị  —   —   — |
```

TODE (VARIATION)

```
(1)   —   —   —   — | Mạ Pa  Nị Sa | Mạ Pa  Nị Sa | Sa  Nị  Ma  |
      Ma  Pa  Nị Sa | Nị Re  Sa  — | Nị Re  Sa  —  | Ga  Ma   —   — |
(2)   —   —   —   — | Mạ Pa  Nị Sa | Pạ Nị Sa  Re | Nị Sa  Re  Ma |
      Ma  Re  Sa  Nị| Pa  Nị Sa  — | Nị Re  Sa  —  | Ga  Ma   —   — |
(3)   —   —   —   — | Nị Sa  Re  Ma| Nị Sa  Re  Ma | Pa  Ma  Re  Sa |
      Pa  Ma  Re  Sa| Nị Re  Sa  — | Ma  Re  Sa  —  | Ga  Ma   —   — |
(4)   —   —   —   — | Nị Sa  Re  Ma| Sa  Re  Ga  Pa | Re  Ma  Pa  Ni |
      Ni  Pa  Ma  Re| Pa  Nị Sa  Re| Nị Sa  Ga  Ma | —   —    —   — |
(5)   —   —   —   — | Nị Sa  Re  Ma| Pa  Nị Sa  —  | Sa  Ni  Pa  Ma |
      Ma  Re  Sa  — | Nị Re  Sa  — | Nị Re  Sa  Ga | Ma  —    —   — |
```

4
RAGH-BAGESHREE

TAL-TRITAL

1	2	3	4		5	6		7	8		9	10	11	12		13	14	15	16	

(1)
| | | | | | | | | | | | | Ga | — | | | Ma | Dha | — | Ni | |

Dha — Ma — | Ga — Ga Ma | Ga Re Sa — | — — — — |

(2)
| | | | | | | | | | | | Ni | — | — | | | Sa | Dha | — | Ni | |

Sa — Ga — | Ma — Dha Ni | Dha — Ma — | — — — — |

(3)
| | | | | | | | | | | | | Ga | — | | | Ma | Dha | — | Ni | |

Dha — — Ga | Ma Dha — Ni | Dha — — Ga | Ma Dha — Ni |

Dha — — — |

Tode (Variation)

(1) — — — — | Dha Ni Sa — | Dha Ni Sa — | Sa Ni Dha Ma |

Ma Dha Ni Sa | Ni Re Sa — | Ni Re Sa Ga Ma—

(2) — — — — | Dha Ni Sa Re | Dha Ni Sa Re | Ga Re Sa Ni |

Ma Dha Ni Sa | Ni Re Sa — | Ga Re Sa Ga Ma—

(3) — — — — | Ni Sa Ga Ma | Sa Ga Ma Ma | Ga Ma Dh Ni |

Dha Ma Ga Re | Dha Ni Sa — | Ni Re Sa \ Ga Ma

(4) — — — — | Ni Sa Ga Ma | Sa Ga Ma Dha | Ma Dha Ni Sa|

Sa Ni Dha Ma | Ga Re Sa — | Ni Re Sa \ Ga Ma

(5) — — — — | Ga Ma Dha Ni | Ma Dha Ni Sa | Ni Re Sa |

Sa Ni Dha Ma | Ga Re Sa — | Dha Ni Sa \ Ga Ma— —

(6) — — — — | Dha Ni Dha Ni | Dha Ni Sa — | Dha Ni Dha Ni |

Dha Ni Sa — | Sa Sa Ni Ni | Dha Dha Ma Ma | Ma Ma Dha Dha

Ni Ni Sa Sa | Ni Re Sa — | Ni Re Sa — | Ga Ma — —

(7) — — — — | Dha Ni Sa Re | Dha Ni Sa Re | Dha Ni Sa Ga |

Ga Re Sa — | Ni Re Sa — | Ni Re Sa \ Ga Ma— —

(8) — — — — | Ni Sa Ga Ma | Ni Sa Ga Ma | Sa Ga Ma Ma |

Sa Ga Ma Ma | Ga Ma Dha Ni | Ga Ma Dha Ni | Dha Ma Ga Re |

Dha Ma Ga Re | Dha Ni Sa — | Ni Re Sa Ga | Ma — — —

(9) — — — — | Ni Sa Ga Ma | Ni Sa Ga Ma | Sa Ga Ma Dha

Sa Ga Ma Dha | Sa Ga Ma Dha | Ma Dha Ni Sa | Ma Dha Ni Sa

Sa Ni Dha Ma | Sa Ni Dha Ma | Ga Re Sa | Ga Ma — — |

(10) — — — — | Ga Ma Dha Ni | Ga Ma Dha Ni | Ma Dha Ni Sa |

Ma Dha Ni Sa | Ni Re Sa — | Ni Re Sa — | Sa Ni Dha Ma |

Sa Ni Dha Ma | Ga Re Sa — | Dha Ni Sa Ga Ma — — |

5
RAGH-BIHAG

TAL-TRITAL

	1	2	3	4	5	6	7	8	9	10	11	12	13	14	15	16
(1)	—	—	—	—	—	—	—	—	—	—	—	—	Ni	Sa	Ga	—
	Pa	—	Mả	Pa	Ga	—	Ga	Ma	Ga	Re	Sa	—	—	—	—	—
(2)	—	—	—	—	—	—	—	—	—	—	—	Ni̱	Sa	Pa	—	Ni
	Sa	—	Ga	—	Ma	—	Ga	Ma	Ga	Re	Sa	—	—	—	—	—
(3)	—	—	—	—	—	—	—	—	Ni̱	Sa	Ga	—	Ma	—		
	Ga	—	—	Ni̱	Sa	Ga	—	Ma	Ga	—	—	Ni̱	—	Ga	—	Ma
(1)	—	—	—	—	—	—	—	—	Sa	Pa	Mả	Pả	—	Ga	—	Ma
	Ga	—	—	—	Re	—	Sa	—								
(2)	—	—	—	—	—	—	—	—	Pạ	—	Pạ	Ni̱	—	Ni̱	Sa	—
	Pa	—	Ma	Pa	Ga	Mả	Ga	—	—	—	—	—				
(3)	—	—	—	—	—	—	—	—	Sa	Pa	Mả	Pa	—	Ga	—	Ma
	Ga	—	—	—												

TODE (VARIATION)

(1)	—	—	—	—	Pa	Ni̱	Sa	Ga	Pạ	Ni̱	Sạ	Ga	Ma	Ga	Re	Sa
	Mả	Ga	Re	Sa	Ga	Mả	Ga	—	Ga	Re	Sa	—	Ga	Ma	—	—
(2)	—	—	—	—	Ni̱	Sa	Ga	Ma	Ni̱	Sạ	Ga	Ma	Pa	Mả	Ga	Ma
	Ga	Re	Sa	—	Pạ	Ni̱	Sa	—	Ni̱	Re	Sa	—	Ga	Ma	—	—
(3)	—	—	—	—	Ni	Sa	Ga	Ma	Sa	Ga	Ma	Pạ	Ga	Ma	Pa	Ni
	Pa	Mả	Ga	Ma	Ga	Re	Sa	—	Ga	Re	Sa	Ga	Ma			
(4)	—	—	—	—	Ga	Ma	Pa	Ni	Ma	Pa	Ni	Sả	Ni	Dha	Pa	Mả
	Ga	Ma	Ga	—	Pa	Ni	Sa	Ga	Ma	—	—	—	—			
(5)	—	—	—	—	Ma	Pa	Ni	Sả	Ma	Pa	Ni	Sa	Gả	Mả	Gả	Rẻ
	Sa	—	—	—	Pa	Ni	Sả	—	Pa	Ni	Sả	Ga	Ma	—	—	—

(6)
RAGH-MALKAUNSE

TAL-TRITAL

1	2	3	4	5	6	7	8	9	10	11	12	13	14	15	16

1) — — — — | — — — — | Ga Ma Ga Sa | Ni Sa Dha Ni |
Ma — Ma — | Dha— Ma — |

2) — — — — — — | Ga —Ma— | Dha — Ni — |
Sa — Sa — | Ga — Sa — | Ni — Ni — | Dha— Dha — |
Ma — Ma — | Ga — Sa — |

3) — — — — | Ga Ma Ga Sa | Ni Sa Dha Ni |
Ma — Ma — | Ga — Sa — |

TODE (VARIATION)

1) — — — — | Ma Dha Ni Sa | Dha Ni Sa — | Sa Ni Dha Ma |
Ma Dha Ni Sa | Ga — Sa — | Ga Ma — — — —

2) — — — — | Dha Ni Sa — | Dha Ni Sa — | Ni Sa Ga Ma |
Ga — Sa — | Dha Ni Sa — | Ga Ma — — — —

3) — — — — | Ni Sa Ga Ma | Sa Ga Ma Dha | DhaMa Ga Sa |
Dha Ma Ga Sa | Ga — Sa — | Ga Ma

4) — — — — | Ni Sa Ga Ma | Sa Ga Ma Dha | Ga Ma Dha Ni |
Dha Ma Ga Sa | Dha Ni Sa — | Ga Ma

5) — — — — | Sa Ga Ma Dha | Ga Ma Dha Ni | Ma Dha Ni Sa |
Sa Ni Dha Ma | Ga — Sa — | Ga Ma

(7)
RAGH-PURIYA KALYAN
OR
PURVA KALYAN

TAL-TRITAL

	1	2	3	4	5	6	7	8	9	10	11	12	13	14	15	16
(1)	—	—	—	—	—	—	—	—	—	—	—	Ni	Re	Ga	—	Ma
	Pa	—	—	—	Ga	—	Má	Ga	Re	—	Sa	—	—	—	—	—
(2)	—	—	—	—	—	—	—	—	—	—	—	Ni	Sa	Dha	—	Ni
	Re	—	Ga	—	Má	—	Dha	Ni	Dha	—	Pa					
(3)	—	—	—	—	—	—	—	—	—	—	—	Ni	Sa	Ga	—	Má
	Pá	—	—	Ni	Sa	Ga	—	Má	Pa	—	—	Ni	Sa	Ga	—	Má
	Pa	—	—	—												

Tode (Variation)

	1	2	3	4	5	6	7	8	9	10	11	12	13	14	15	16
(1)	—	—	—	—	Dha	Ni	Sa	Sa	Dha	Ni	Sa	Sa	Ni	Re	Sa	—
	Ni	Re	Sa	—	Dha	Ni	Sa	—	Ga	Re	Sa	Ga	Ma	—	—	—	—
(2)	—	—	—	—	Dha	Ni	Sa	Re	Ni	Sa	Re	Re	Sa	Re	Ga	Ga
	Re	Ma	Ma	Ga	Ni	Re	Sa	—	Dha	Ni	Sa	—	Ga	Ma	—	—
(3)	—	—	—	—	Sa	Re	Ga	Má	Re	Ga	Má	Pa	Ga	Má	Pa	
	Má	Ga	Re	Sa	Ni	Re	Sa	—	Ni	Re	Sa	Ga	Ma	—	—	—
(4)	—	—	—	—	Re	Ga	Má	Pa	Ga	Má	Pa	Pa	Má	Dha	Pa	—
	Dha	Pa	Má	Ga	Má	Ga	Re	Sa	Ni	Re	Sa	Ga	Ma	—	—	—
(5)	—	—	—	—	Ga	Ma	Dha	Ni	Ma	Dha	Ni	Sá	Sá	Ni	Dha	Pa
	Má	Ga	Re	Sa	Dha	Ni	Sa	—	Ni	Re	Sa	Ga	Ma	—	—	—

(8)
RAGH-DARBARI KANNADA

TAL-TRITAL

1	2	3	4	5	6	7	8	9	10	11	12	13	14	15	16
—	—	—	—	—	—	—	—	Re	—	Re	Re	—	Re	Sa	Re

Ga — Ga Ma | Re — Dha Ni | — — — — — — —

| — | — | — | — | — | — | — | — | Sa | — | Re | Ga | — | Ma | Pa | — |

Ga — Ga Ma | Re — Sa — |

| — | — | — | — | — | — | — | — | Re | — | Re | Re | — | Re | Sa | Re |

Re — Re Re | — Re Sa Re | Re — Re Re | — Re Sa Re |

a — Ga Ma | Re — Sa — |

Tode (Variation)

| — | — | — | — | — | — | — | — | Dha Dha | Ni | Sa | | Dha Dha | Ni | Sa | |

Ni Sa Re Re | Dha Ni Sa — | Ga Ma

| — | — | — | — | — | — | — | — | Ni | Ni | Sa | Re | Ni Ni | Sa | Re | |

Ga — Ga Ma | Re — Sa — | Ga Ma — — — —

| — | — | — | — | — | — | — | — | Sa | Re | Ga | Ma | Re | Ga | Ma | Pa |

Ga — Ga Ma | Re Sa Ni Sa | Ga · Ma

| — | — | — | — | — | — | — | — | Ma | Pa | Dha Dha | | Ni | Ni | Pa | Pa |

Dha — Ni Sa | Dha Ni Sa — | Ga Ma — — — —

| — | — | — | — | — | — | — | — | Sa | Re | Ga | Ma | Pa | Dha | Ni | Sa |

Sa DhaNi Pa | Ga Ma Re Sa | Ga Ma — — — — — —

(9)

RAGH-MIYA MALHAR

TAL-TRITA

1	2	3	4	5	6	7	8	9	10	11	12	13	14	15	16
(1) —	—	—	—	—	—	—	—	Ga	Ma	Re	Sa	Ni	Dha	Ni	Sa
Ma	Pa	Ni	Dha	DhaNi		Ni	Sa								
(2) —	—	—	—	—	—	—	—	Pa	—	Pa	Pa	Ni	—	Pa	—
Ga	Ma	Re	Sa	Ni	Dha	Ni	Sa								
(3) —	—	—	—	—	—	—	—	Ga	Ma	Re	Sa	Ni	Dha	Ni	Sa
Ga	Ma	Re	Sa	Ni	Dha	Ni	Sa	Ga	Ma	Re	Sa	Ni	Dha	Ni	Sa

Tode (Variation)

(1) Ma	Pa	Ni	Dha	Ni	—	Sa	—	Ni	Dha	Ni	Sa	Dha—		Ni	Sa
Dha	Ni	Sa	Sa	Ni	Dha	Pa	—	Ga	Ma						
(2) Ni	Sa	Re	—	Sa	Re	Pa	—	Ga	—	Ga	Ma	Ma	Re	Sa	—
Ga	—	Ga	Ma	Ma	Re	Sa	—	Ga	Ma	—	—	—	—		
(3) Sa	Re	Pa	Pa	Ga	Ma	Re	Sa	Sa	Re	Pa	Pa	Ni	Dha	Pa	—
Ga	Ma	Re	Pa	Ni	Dha	Pa	—	Ga	Ma	—	—	—	—		
(4) Ga	Ma	Re	Pa	Ni	Dha	Pa	—	Ma	Pa	Dha	Ni	DhaNi		Sá	—
Ni	Dha	Ma	Pa	Ga	Ma	Re	Sa	Ga	Ma	—	—	—	—		
(5) Ma	Pa	Ni	Dha	Ni	—	Sa	—	Ga	Ma	Re	Sa	DhaNi		Sa	—
Sa	Ni	—	Pa	Ga	Ma	Re	Sa	Ga	Ma	—	—	—			

(10)
RAGH BHAIRAV

TAL-DADRA
(6 BEATS)

	1	2	3			4	5	6				
)	Ma	Ma	—	|		Pa	Pa	—	|			
	Dha	Dha	Dha	|		Ma	Pa	Ga	|			
)	Ma	Ma	—	|		Ga	Ga	—	|			
	Sa	Re	Ga	|		Sa	Re	Dha	|			
	Sa	—	—	|		Sa	—	—	|			

Tode (Variation)

	1	2	3			4	5	6				
)	Dha	—	—	|		Sa	Sa	—	|			
	Re	—	—	|		Sa	Sa	—	|			
	Ma	—	—	|		Ga	—	—	|			
	Re	—	—	|		Sa	Sa	—	|			
	Ni	—	—	|		Sa	Sa	—	|			
	Re	—	—	|		Sa	Sa	—	|	Ga	Ma	—
)	Dha	Ni	Sa	|		Dha	Ni	Sa	|			
	Re	Ga	Re	|		Ni	Re	Sa	|			
	Re	Ga	Ma	|		Ga	Ma	Pa	|			
	Pa	Ma	Ga	|		Ma	Re	Sa	|			
	Dha	Ni	Sa	|		Ni	Re	Sa	|	Ga	Ma	—
)	Sa	Re	Ga	|		Re	Ga	Ma	|			
	Ga	Ma	Pa	|		Ma	Pa	Dha	|			
	Ma	Dha	Pa	|		Ga	Pa	Ma	|			
	Re	Ma	Ga	|		Ni	Re	Sa	|	Ga	Ma	—
)	Ga	Ma	Pa	|		Ma	Pa	Dha	|			
	Pa	Dha	Ni	|		Dha	Ni	Sa̍	|			
	Sa̍	Ni	Dha	|		Dha	Ni	Sa̍	|			
	Dha	Pa	Ma	|		Ga	Re	Sa	|	Ga	Ma	—
)	Ma	Pa	Dha	|		Dha	Ni	Sa̍	|			

Ni	Re	Sa	|	Sȧ	Re	Ga	|
Re	Ga	Ma	|	Ma	Ga	Re	|
Ga	Re	Sa	|	Sa	Ni	Dha	|
Ni	Dha	Pa	|	Dha	Pa	Ma	|
Ga	Re	Sa	|	Dha	Ni	Dha	|

1) यमन

आरोह	:-	नि	रे	ग	म	ध	नी	सां।
अवरोह	:-	सां	नि	ध	म	ग	रे	सा।

2) भूप

आरोह	:-	सा	रे	ग	–	प	ध	सां।
अवरोह	:-	सा	ध	प	ग	रे	सा	।

3) बिंदावनी सारंग

आरोह	:-	सा	रे	म	प	नी	सां	।
अवरोह	:-	सां	नि	प	म	रे	सा	।

(4) बागेश्री

आरोह	:-	सा	ग॒	म	ध	नी॒	सां	।
अवरोह	:-	सां	नि॒	ध	म	ग॒रे	सा	।

(5) बिहाग

आरोह	:-	नि॒	सा	ग	म	प	नी	सां	।		
अवरोह	:-	सां	नीं	ध	प	मं	प	ग	म	ग	रे	सा।

(6) मालकंस

आरोह	:-	सा	ग	म	ध॒	नी॒	सां	।
अवरोह	:-	सां	नि॒	ध॒	म	ग॒	सां	।

(7) पुरिया कल्याण (पुर्वा कल्याण)

आरोह	सा	रे	म	मं	प	ध्	नि॒	सां	।	
अवरोह	सां	नि॒	ध	प	म	ग	रे	सा	।	

(8) दरबारी कानडा

आरोह	सा	–	रे	ग॒	म	प	ध्	नि॒	सां	।	
अवरोह	सां	ध्	नि॒	प	म	प	ग॒	म	रे	सा	।

(9) मियों मल्हार

आरोह	सा	रे	ग॒	प	म	प	नि॒	ध	नि	सां	।
अवरोह	सां	ध	नि॒	प	म	प	ग॒	म	रे	सा	।

(10) भैरवी

आरोह	सा	रे॒	ग॒	म	प	ध॒	नी॒	सां	।
अवरोह	सा	नि॒	ध॒	प	म	ग॒	रे॒	सा	।

राग-यमन　　　　　　　　　　　　　　ताल-त्रिताल

1	2	3	4		5	6	7	8		9	10	11	12		13	14	15	16	
												नि			रे	ग		रे	
ग	–	–	–		ग	रे	ग	मं		ग	रे	सा	–						
										नि		रे	ग	–	रे				
ग	–	मं	–		प	–	मं	–		रे	–	सा							
										नि		रे	ग	–	रे				
ग	–	–	नि		रे	ग	–	रे		ग	–	–	नि		रे	ग	–	रे	
ग	–	–																	

तोडे (व्हेरिएशन)

(1) – – – – । मं ध् नि सा । मं ध् नि सा । सा नि ध् प ।
मं ध् नि सा । नि रे सा – । नि रे सा गा । गम . . . . ।

(2) – – – – । मं ध नि सा । ध् नि सा रे । रे सा नि ध् ।
मं ध नि सा । नि रे सा – । नि रे सा गम . . . .

(3) – – – – । नि रे ग मं । रे ग मं प । प मं ग रे ।
म ग रे सा । नि रे सा – । ध नि सा – । ग म . . . .

(4) – – – – । नि रे ग ग । नि रे ग गम . . . . .
मं ग रे सा । मं ध् निं सा । नि रे सा – । ग म . . .

(5) – – – – । नि रे ग मं । रे ग मं प । ग मं प ध ।
प मं ग रे । म ध नि सा । नि रे सा – । गम . . . .

(6) – – – – । नि रे ग मं । ध नि सा – । सां नि ध प ।
मं ग रे सा । नि रे सां नि । रे सा – गम . .

(2) राग-भूप　　　　　　　　　(ताल-त्रिताल)

	1	2	3	4		5	6	7	8		9	10	11	12		13	14	15	16	
(1)	1	2	3	4	।	5	6	7	8	।	ग	प	ग	रे	।	सा	ध्	सा	रे	
(2)	ग	–	–	–	।	ग	रे	सा	–	।	–	–	–							
										।	ध	ध	सा	–	।	ध	ध	सा	–	।
(3)	–	–	–	–	।	–	–	–	–	।	म	प	ग	रे	।	सा	ध	सा	रे	।

ग॑ प ग रे सा ध् सा रे ग प ग रे – । सा ध् सा रे ।

तोडे (व्हेरिएशन)

	1	2	3	4		5	6	7	8		9	10	11	12		13	14	15	16	
(1)	–	–	–	–	।	प॒	ध॒	सा॑	रे	।	प॒	ध॒	सा	रे	।	रे	सा	ध	प	।

प॒ ध॒ सा रे । ध॒ रे सा – । गम . . . . . .

(2)	–	–	–	–	।	प॒	ध॒	सा	रे	।	ध॒	सा॑	रे	ग	।	ग	रे	सा	ध॒	।

रे सा ध प । ध रे सा – । गम . . . .

(3)	–	–	–	–	।	सा	रे	ग	ग	।	सा	रे	ग	ग	।	रे	ग	प	प	।

रे ग प प । प ग रे सा । गम . . . . .

(4)	–	–	–	–	।	सा	रे	ग	प	।	रे	ग	प	प	।	प	ग	रे	सा	।

प ध सा रे । ग रे सा – । गम . . . . . .

(5)	–	–	–	–	।	सा	रे	ग	प	।	ध	ध	सां	–	।	सां	ध	प	ग	।

ग रे सा – । ध रे सा – । गम . . . . . .

(3) राग-सारंग (ब्रिंदावनी)   ताल त्रिताल

1   2   3   4 । 5   6   7   8 । 9   10   11   12 । 13   14   15   16 ।

म । रे नि॒ – सा ।

(1) नि॒ – – – । प – नि – । रे – सा – । ग म – – ।

नि । सा प – नी॒ ।

(2) सा – रे – । म – प म । रे – सा

(3)   म । रे नि॒ – सा ।

नि॒ – – म । रे नि॒ – सा । नि॒ – – म । रे नि॒ – सा ।

नि॒ – – – ।

तोडे (व्हेरिएशन)

(1) – – – – । म॒ प॒ नि॒ सा । म॒ प॒ नि॒ सा । सा नि॒ प म ।

म प नि सा । नि॒ रे सा – । नि॒ रे सा – । ग म..... ।

(2) – – – – । म प नि सा । प॒ नि॒ सा रे । नि॒ सा रे म ।

म रे सा नि॒ । प॒ नि॒ सा – । नि॒ रे सा गन...... ।

(3) – – – – । नि॒ सा रे म । नि॒ सा रे म । प म रे सा ।

प म रे सा । नि॒ रे सा – । म रे सा गन...... ।

(4) – – – – । नि॒ सा रे म । सा रे म प । रे म प नि॒ ।

नि॒ प म रे । प॒ नि॒ सा रे । नि॒ रे सा ग म...... ।

(5) – – – – । नि॒ सा रे म । प नि सां – । सां नि॒ प म ।

म रे सा – । नि॒ रे सा – । नि॒ रे सा – । गन....... ।

(4) राग बागेश्री (ताल त्रिताल)

1	2	3	4	5	6	7	8	9	10	11	12	13	14	15	16

(1)
| | | | | | | | | | | | ग् | म | क | – | नी |

| ध | – | म | – | ग् | – | ग् | म | ग् | रे | सा | – | – | – | – | – |

| | | | | | | | | | | | नि | सा | ध | – | नी |

(2)
| सा | – | ग् | – | म | – | ध | नी | ध | – | म | – | . | . | . | . |

| | | | | | | | | | | | ग् | म | ध | – | नी |

| ध | – | – | ग् | म | ध | – | नी | ध | – | – | ग् | म | ध | – | नी |

| ध | – | – | – |

तोडे (व्हेरिएशन)

(1)
| – | – | – | – | ध् | नि | सा | – | ध् | नि | सा | – | सा | नि | ध् | म् |

| म् | ध् | नि | सा | नि | रे | सा | – | नि | रे | सा | – | ग | म | . | . |

(2)
| – | – | – | – | ध | नि | सा | रे | ध् | नि | सा | रे | ग् | रे | सा | नि |

| म् | ध् | नि | सा | नि | रे | सा | – | ग् | रे | सा | – | ग | म | . | . |

(3)
| – | – | – | – | नि | सा | ग् | म | सा | ग् | म | म | ग् | म | क | नी |

| ध | म् | गे | रे | ध | नि | सा | – | नि | रे | सा | – | ग | म | . | . |

(4)
| – | – | – | – | नि | सा | ग् | म | सा | ग् | म | ध | म | क | नी | सां |

| सा | नि | ध | म | ग् | रे | सा | – | नि | रे | सा | – | ग | म | . | . |

(5)
| – | – | – | – | ग् | म | ध | नी | म | ध | नी | सां | नि | रे | सां | – |

| सां | नि | ध | म | ग् | रे | सा | – | ध | नि | सा | – | ग | म | . | . |

(6)
| – | – | – | – | ध | नि | ध | नि | ध | नि | सा | – | ध | नि | ध | नि |

| ध | नि | सा | – | सा | सा | नि | नि | ध | ध | म् | म् | म् | म् | ध् | ध् |

| नि | नि | सा़ | सा | नि | रे | सा | – | नि | रे | सा | – | ग | म | . | . |

(7)
| – | – | – | – | ध | नि | सा | रे | ध | नि | सा | रे | ध | नि | सा | ग् |

| ग् | रे | सा | – | नि | रे | सा | – | नि | रे | सा | – | ग | म | . | . |

(8) – – – – । नि॒ सा ग॒ म । नि॒ सा ग॒ म । सा ग॒ म म ।
सा ग॒ म म । ग॒ म ध नि॒ । ग म ध नि॒ । ध म ग॒ रे ।
ध म ग॒ रे । ध॒ नि सा – । नि॒ रे सा – । ग म . . . . . . ।

(9) – – – – । नि॒ सा ग॒ म । नि॒ सा ग॒ म । सा ग॒ म ध ।
सा ग॒ म क । सा ग॒ म ध । म ध नि॒ सां । म ध नि॒ सां ।
सा नि॒ ध म । सां नि॒ ध म । ग॒ रे सा – । ग म . . . . . . ।

(10) – – – – । ग॒ म ध नि॒ । ग॒ म ध नि॒ । म ध नि॒ सा ।
म ध नि॒ सा । नि॒ रे सा – । नि॒ रें सा – । सा नि॒ ध म ।
सा नि॒ ध म । ग॒ रे सा – । ध नि॒ सा – । ग म . . . . . . ।

(5) राग - बिहाग (ताल त्रिताल)

1	2	3	4		5	6	7	8		9	10	11	12		13	14	15	16	

(1) — — — — । — — — — । — — — — । नि सा ग — ।
प — मं प । ग — ग म । ग रे सा

(2) — — — — । — — — — । — — — नि । सा पे — नि ।
सां — ग — । म — ग म । ग रे सा नि । सा प — नि ।

(3) — — — — । — — — — । — — — नि । सा ग — म ।
ग — — नि । सा ग — म । ग — — नि । सा ग — म ।
ग — — — । रे सा ।

गन 2 रो

(1) — — — — । — — — — । सा प मं प । — ग — म ।
ग — — — । रे — सा — ।

(2) — — — — । — — — — । प॒ — प॒ नि॒ । — नि॒ सा — ।
प — मं प । ग म ग — । — — — — । — — — — ।

(3) — — — — । — — — — । सा प मे प । — ग — म ।
ग — — — ।

तोडे (व्हेरिएशन)

(1) — — — — । प नि॒ सा ग । प॒ नि॒ सा ग । म ग रे सा ।
मं ग रे सा । ग मं ग — । ग रे सा — । ग म .... ।

(2) — — — — । नि॒ सा ग म । नि॒ सा॒ ग म । प मं ग म ।
ग रे सा — । प॒ नि॒ सा — । नि॒ रे सा — । ग म .... ।

(3) — — — — । नि सा ग म । सा ग म प॒ । ग म प नी ।
प मं ग म । ग रे सा — । ग रे सा — । ग म ..... ।

(4) — — — — । ग म प नी । म प नि सां । नि क प मं ।
ग म ग — । प नि सा — । ग म .....।

(5) — — — — । प नि सां — । म प नि सां । गं मं गं रें ।

सां – – – । प नि सां – प नि सां ग म......

(6) मालकंस　　　　　　　　　　　ताल त्रिताल

1	2	3	4	।	5	6	7	8	।	9	10	11	12	।	13	14	15	16	।

(1) – – – – । – – – – । ग् म ग् सा । नि॒ सा ध् नि॒ ।

म – म – । ध् – म – ।

(2) 　　　　　　　। ग् – म – । ध् – नि॒ – ।

सां – सां – । गं – सा – । नि॒ – नि॒ – । ध् – ध् – ।

म – म – । ग् – सा – ।

(3) – – – – । – – – 　। ग् म ग् सा । नि॒ सा क् नि॒ ।

ग् म ग् सा । नि॒ सा ध् नि॒ । ग् म ग् सा । नि॒ सा ध् नि॒ ।

म – म – । ग – सा – ।

तोडे (व्हेरिएश्न)

(1) – – – – । म ध् नि॒ सा । ध् नि॒ सा – । सा नि॒ ध् म ।

म॒ ध् नि॒ सा । ग् – सा – । ग म...... ।

(2) – – – – । ध नि सा – । ध् नि सा – । नि॒ सा ग् म ।

ग् – सा – । ध् नि॒ सा – । ग म...... ।

(3) – – – – । नि॒ सा ग् म । सा ग् म ध् । ध् म ग् सा ।

ध् म ग् सा । ग् – सा – । ग म...... ।

(4) – – – – । नि॒ सा ग् म । सा ग् म ध् । ग् म ध् नि॒ ।

ध् म ग् सा । ध् नि सा – । ग म......। ।

(5) – – – – । सा ग् म ध् । ग् म ध् नी । म ध् नि॒ सां ।

सां नि ध म । ग् – सा – । ग म...... ।

(7) पुरिया कल्याण (पुर्वा कल्याण) ताल त्रिताल

```
      1   2   3   4  | 5   6   7   8  | 9   10  11  12 | 13  14  15  16 |
(1)   -   -   -   -  | -   -   -   -  | -   -   -  नि॒ | रे॒  ग   -   म  |
      प   -   -   -  | ग   -  मं   ग  | रे  -  सा   -  | -   -   -   -  |
(2)   -   -   -   -  | -   -   -   -  | -   -   -  नि॒ | स  ध॒   ग   म  |
      रे॒  -   ग   -  | म   -   ध  नी  | ध   -   प
(3)   -   -   -   -  | -   -   -   -  | -   -   -  नि॒ | सा   ग   -   म  |
      पं  -   -  नि॒ | सा   ग   -  मे  | प   -   -  नि॒ | सा   ग   -  म॑  |
      प   -   -  -  |
```

तोडे (व्हेरिएशन)

```
(1)   -   -   -   -  | ध॒  नि॒ सा  सा | ध॒  नि॒ सा  सा | नि॒ रे॒ सा   -  |
      नि॒ रे॒ सा   -  | ध॒  नि॒ सा   - | ग   रे॒ सा   -  | ग   म.....     |
(2)   -   -   -   -  | ध   नि  सा  रे॒ | नि॒ सा  रे॒  रे॒ | सा  रे॒  ग   ग  |
      रे॒  म  मं   ग  | नि  रे॒ सा   -  | ध॒  नि  सा   - | ग   म......    |
(3)   -   -   -   -  | सा  रे   ग   म  | रे॒  ग   म   प | ग   मे   प   -  |
      मं   ग  रे॒ सा  | नि॒ रे॒ सा   -  | नि॒ रे॒ सा   - | ग   म.....     |
(4)   -   -   -   -  | रे॒  ग  मं   प | ग  मं   प   प  | मं  ध   प   -  |
      ध   प  मं   ग  | मं   ग  रे॒ सा  | नि॒ रे॒ सा   -  | ग   म......    |
(5)   -   -   -   -  | ग   मे  ध  नी  | मे  ध  नी  सां | सां नि  ध   प  |
      मं   ग  रे॒ सा  | ध॒  नि॒ सा   -  | नि॒ रे॒ सा   - | म   म.. ....   |
```

(8) राग दरबारी कानडा (ताल त्रिताल)

1	2	3	4	5	6	7	8	9	10	11	12	13	14	15	16
(1) –	–	–	–	–	–	–	–	रे	–	रे	रे	–	रे	सा	रे

ग् – ग् म । रे – ध नि ।

| (2) – | – | – | – | – | – | – | – | सा | – | रे | ग् | – | म | प | – |

ग् – ग् म । रे – सा – ।

| (3) – | – | – | – | – | – | – | – | रे | – | रे | रे | – | रे | सा | रे |

रे – रे रे । – रे सा रे । रे रे सा रे ।

ग् – ग् म । रे – सा – ।

तोडे (व्हेरिएशन)

| (1) – | – | – | – | – | – | – | – | धू धू | नि | सा | धू | धू | नि् | सा |

नि सा रे रे । धू नि सा – । ग म . . . . . ।

| (2) | | | | | | | | नि् नि् | सा | रे | नि् | नि् | सा | रे |

ग् – ग् म । रे – सा – । ग म . . . . . . ।

| (3) – | – | – | – | – | – | – | – | सा रे | ग् | म | रे | ग् | म | प |

ग् – ग् म । रे सा नि् सा । ग म . . . . . ।

| (4) – | – | – | – | – | – | – | – | म प | ध् | ध् | नि् | नि् | प | प |

– ध् नि् सां । ध् नि् सां – । ग म . . . . . . ।

| (5) – | – | – | – | – | – | – | – | सा रे | ग् | म | प | ध् | नि् | सां |

सां ध नी् प । ग् म रे सा । ग म . . . . . . ।

(9) राग मियाँ मल्हार ताल त्रिताल

| 1 | 2 | 3 | 4 | | 5 | 6 | 7 | 8 | | 9 | 10 | 11 | 12 | | 13 | 14 | 15 | 16 | |

(1) – – – – । – – – – । ग॒ म रे सा । नि॒ ध॒ नि॒ सा ।

म॑ प॒ नि॒ ध । ध॒ नि॒ नि॒ सा ।

(2) । प – प प । नि॒ – प – ।

ग॒ म रे सा । नि॒ ध नि सा ।

(3) – – – – । – – – – । ग॒ म रे सा । नि॒ ध॒ नि॒ सा ।

ग॒ मे रे सा । नि॒ ध॒ नि॒ सा । ग॒ म रे सा । नि॒ ध॒ नि॒ सा ।

तोडे (व्हेरिएशन)

(1) म॑ प॒ नि॒ ध । नि॒ – सा – । नि॒ ध नि॒ सा । ध – नि सा ।

ध नि सा सा । नि ध प – । ग म . . . . ।

(2) नि॒ सा रे – । सा रे प – । ग॒ – ग॒ म । म रे सा – ।

ग॒ – ग॒ म । म रे सा – । ग म ।

(3) सा रे प प । ग॒ म रे सा । सा रे प प । नि॒ ध प – ।

ग॒ म रे प । नि॒ ध प – । ग म . . . . . . ।

(4) ग॒ म रे प । नि॒ ध प – । म प ध नी॒ । ध नि सां – ।

नि॒ ध म प । ग॒ म रे सा । ग म . . . . . ।

(5) म प नि॒ क । नि – सां – । गं॒ मं रें सां । क नि सां – ।

सां नि॒ – प । ग॒ म रे सा । ग म . . . . . . ।

(10) भैरवी (ताल दादरा)

1	2	3	।	4	5	6	।
(1) म	म	–	।	प	प	–	।
ध्	ध्	ध्	।	प	म	ग्	।
(2) म	म	–	।	ग्	ग्	–	।
सा	रे॒	ग्	।	सा	रे	ध	।
सा	–	–	।	सा	–	–	।

तोडे (व्हेरिएशन)

(1) ध्॒	–	–	।	सा	सा	–	।
रे॒	–	–	।	सा	सा	–	।
म	–	–	।	ग्	–	–	।
रे॒	–	–	।	सा	सा	–	।
नि	–	–	।	सा	सा	–	।
रे॒	–	–	।	सा	सा	–	।ग. . . .म . . . . .
(2) ध्॒	नि॒	सा	।	ध्॒	नि॒	सा	।
ग्	ग्	रे॒	।	नि॒	रे॒	सा	।
रे॒	ग्	म	।	ग्	म	प	।
प	म	ग्	।	म	रे	सा	।
ध्॒	नि॒	सा	।	नि	रे॒	सा	।ग. . . . . म . . . .
(3) सा	रे॒	ग्	।	रे॒	ग्	म	।
ग्	म	प	।	म	प	ध्	।
म	ध्	प	।	ग्	प	म	।
रे॒	म	ग्	।	नि॒	रे॒	सा	।ग. . . .म . . . .
(4) ग्	म	प	।	म	प	क्॒	।
प	ध्	नि॒	।	ध्	नि॒	सां	।
सां	नि॒	क्॒	।	नि॒	ध्॒	प	।
ध्॒	प	म	।	ग	रे॒	सा	।ग. . .म . . .
(5) म	प	ध्॒	।	क्॒	नि॒	सा	।
नि॒	रें॒	सां	।	सां	रे	गें	।

रें	ग	म	।	म	ग्	रें	।
ग	रे	सा	।	सा	नि्	ध्	।
नि	ध्	प	।	ध	प	म	।
ग्	रें	सा	।	ध्	नि्	सा	।